THE Coldest Love

SHE'S EVER KNOWN

Books by Leo Sullivan

Life

Innocent

Gangster's Daughter

A Gangsta Chick

Books by Leo Sullivan and Porscha Sterling

Gangland

Keisha & Trigga

Gunplay & LeTavia

THE *Coldest Love*

SHE'S EVER KNOWN

LEO SULLIVAN

KENSINGTON PUBLISHING CORP.

www.kensingtonbooks.com

Dedication

This book is dedicated to the readers who have stood by me throughout the years, always showing your support no matter what.

And to my family. I love you.

Acknowledgments

First, I would like to thank God Almighty for blessing me with the ability to write and helping me on my literary journey.

To my family: None of this would be possible without my beautiful wife, Vera Sullivan. I would never be able to soar if you weren't the wind beneath my wings. I love you for life. My sons, Alphonzo (Toot) and my boogerman, Kingston. And thank you to my wonderful mother-in-law, Lynn. If it hadn't been for your enduring love and support, a lot of things wouldn't be possible. I love you! Thanks to my auntie, Toni Sullivan, for always being supportive of me, and to my friend, Michael Hallmon and his beautiful wife, Sherri Hallmon. I appreciate having you all in my life. To Taya R. Baker: I am truly blessed to have a strong black sista in my life as a best friend and confidante. Thank you!

To my angel in heaven, my dearest Mom. I wish you were here right now, but I know you're here in spirit. I love you forever.

Thank you to my business partners: Adi Cohen, Len Gibson, Wayne Overstreet. I can't wait to see what all we have coming down the line. It's been a wonderful and amazing experience working with you all already.

To my mentor: Dr. Mutulu Shakur. You instilled in me the true sense of our struggle as an oppressed people. It was you that breathed a revolutionary fire into my mind. It was an honor to have you as a mentor and best friend for so long. Free Mutulu!

To Tina Nance: Thank you so much for all that you do (which is a lot!). We've gone through many ups and downs together as we endured the twists, turns and changes in the book industry, but you've always held me down. I'm forever thankful and grateful for you.

To my readers: I love you all! Your show of love gives me the strength and inspiration to keep going. Thank you for your passion for reading and your faith in me to deliver a project that you'll enjoy. And thanks for supporting my film (Summer Madness, available now. Smile…). I've got one film down and many more on the horizon. Thanks for your undying support!

Table of Contents

～

THE *Coldest Love*
SHE'S EVER KNOWN

Chapter One

Sunday

I sat on the couch with my legs barely crossed. My belly was mammoth being that I was eight months pregnant. I wore a pair of my fiancé's boxer shorts over my panties, along with his t-shirt, marinated with the scent of his cologne, as he, Caesar, sat across from me. He was frustrated, for some reason that I didn't yet know.

I took joy at seeing his handsome face scowling with agitation as he, once again, dipped his hand into the pound of loud, a blunt smoldering from his lips. He wasn't wearing a shirt; the apartment was humid and hot because the air condition was barely working, and the landlord really didn't give a fuck.

"Sunday, there are sixteen ounces in a pound, and 28.35 grams in an ounce. You gotta use this scale to measure or just take from the stash that is already bagged up."

He pointed, jabbing with his finger.

"It was only a little bit over because I measured it with my hands. Besides, Kelly is my girl so it's cool."

He wiggled his head. "No! that is what the scale is for. You can't just be diggin' yo' fuckin' hand in the bag, measuring the weed. Da fuck wrong with you, man!"

"I saw you do it," I quipped and then watched his lips turn up at the corners.

"I only do that shit when they spend extra money. That's the only time I give them a little extra."

"Humph! Well, how I'm 'posed to know? I ain't no drug dealer," I replied then shuddered when the baby started kicking and moving around like a miniature earthquake in my stomach. You could see the baby's movement underneath my shirt. Caesar saw it, too. Fascinated by the sight of his baby boy, he hopped up off the loveseat and ran around the table and sat next to me.

"That shit don't hurt?" he asked, rubbing my belly affectionately as the blunt burned in his other hand.

I crinkled my nose from the potent weed smoke and replied.

"A little but not really. It's just a weird feeling."

I watched, feeling my love for him grow as he continued to rub my belly like it was a trophy. Then out of the blue he asked me something as he sucked hard on the blunt.

"Where is the money from the ounce you sold your girl, Kelly?"

A sheepish expression crossed my face.

"Uhhh... I gave it to her on credit," I answered, apprehensively, fully prepared for what I knew would come next.

"CREDIT! That bitch ain't got a job. She ain't got no money! She be hustlin' niggas for a living and running game and now she done hustled yo' friendly ass. A zone costs three hundred and our rent is twelve-fifty but you over here givin' away weed, like that shit charity for broke bitches."

"She gon' pay me back," I protested, knowing in my heart I had possibly made a big mistake. "But Kelly is my girl so... I may have kinda told her that she could have it."

He gave me a blank look and I squirmed nervously under his gaze.

"You know what? Yo' ass fired. First day on the job and yo' ass already fucked up. You fired!" Caesar fumed with disgust, the blunt still burning in his hand.

A halo of smoke formed around his handsome face as he scowled at me like he had bit into a bitter lemon. I don't know what it was but, for some reason, I couldn't help but bust out laughing. Maybe I had got a contact high from the weed. I didn't know what it was, but that shit was hilarious.

At first, he just looked at me with a contemptuous frown and that only made me laugh harder.

"I'm fired? On the first damn day..." I cracked with more giddy laughter.

Soon, he couldn't help but smirk back at me, his eyes slanted and red. Then he smiled and it segued into sumptuous laughter, loud and vibrant, as he embraced me. I fell into his arms and he held me tight, rubbing on my bulging belly. We laughed until my face hurt.

Caesar and I didn't have much and, in the eyes of the world, we weren't worth much either. We were just two kids growing up in the hood, making a way the only way we knew how. In another world, Caesar could have been a shrewd businessman; he was good with numbers and could solve any equation you gave him off the top of his head. I could have probably been a doctor or a lawyer, being that I had what my mama called "an elephant's memory." All I had to do was see something once and I would remember it for life. It was that memory and my beauty that made all the dope boys want me.

"You a sorry ass employee," Caesar teased.

I could feel his heartbeat as I rested my head against his brawny masculine chest. He continued to rub my belly. We enjoyed this precious moment together as the blunt burned between his fingers and the music from his phone played the Drake station on Pandora.

"Nah, but for real, ma, we have to continue to stack these chips. I gotta move you and the baby outta here. I'm tryin' to do it quick... like before you even have the baby. I don't want my son growin' up in this bullshit, I have my stash in the closet getting bigger and bigger, keep playin' and I'ma fuck round and get us a house," he spoke from his heart as he rocked me in his arms.

"I know. But we gon' be fine, bae," I cooed. Enraptured, I laid back and felt the fremitus of his chest as his heart seemed to beat in a rhythm close to mine. But then, suddenly, a thought occurred to me.

"What about Kirk?"

Kirk was Caesar's older brother by three years though, after meeting him, you'd think Caesar was the oldest. Kirk was a gentle giant; he stood about six-fee-six with an affable personality, a naturally good spirit. He was kind of slow in the thinking department, but his heart was pure as gold. He had been staying with us ever since he had come home from prison, about a year ago. The plan had been to let him stay for a month, then that turned into two, then three. The next thing I knew, it was eternity.

I never complained because, with time, I learned to really like Kirk. He was just a big lovable oaf. He helped out around the apartment, contributed money that he earned from washing cars and odd jobs, and otherwise stayed out the way, except whenever I needed him to help with the groceries or fix a running toilet, which was more than Caesar would ever do on his best day.

Kirk was sent to prison for something stupid. He was standing in the trap when Federal agents raided the spot. Someone tossed drugs near him and he was charged for it. His lawyer, a public defender with too many cases to handle and not enough resources to do it, talked him into pleading guilty to three years instead of going to trial, facing fifteen-to-life.

"Kirk is going to have to get his own place or something," Caesar said with shrug.

I looked up at him, appalled. He knew that his brother was a little slow and it would be difficult for him to fend for himself on his own.

"Or... he can stay with us," I beamed and reached over to rub his six-pack abs, trying to place his mind at ease.

Deep down, I knew he didn't want to leave Kirk on his own. It wasn't a secret that ever since they were young boys, Caesar had been taking care of Kirk after their mom was placed in a mental institution. They were inseparable and I didn't want to be the reason that he felt the need to leave Kirk on his own. Maybe another woman could be that heartless but not me.

The baby kicked again and, this time, Caesar sat the blunt down and moved around so that he was facing me.

He grabbed my stomach with the palms of his hands like he was holding the Earth and looked right into it as he declared, "This little nigga gonna be a football player. See how he moving around, kickin' and shit.? We gon' name him Odell Beckham—"

I sucked my teeth disdain. He must've lost his mind.

"I'm not namin' my baby no damn 'Odell'. That sounds like a slave name. People will look at him like, 'what was his mama thinkin'?'" I snapped with a roll of my eyes.

"Odell Beckham is a beast. OBJ... he's a football player."

"I don't care! You need to think of something traditional like 'Caesar Jr.' or at least somethin' civilized. Slave names are dead—out of style. You ain't get the memo?" I gibed and watched Caesar smirk with his eyes slanted, red and sexy.

"So you got jokes now?" He smiled and I couldn't help but admire his flat, muscular stomach along with the fine, silky pubescent hairs that cascaded down his torso into his sweatpants.

Out of spite, I dug my hand inside his pants and grabbed his dick. He flinched, when I folded my hand tightly around it. I'd caught him off-guard. It had been weeks since we last had sex. For some reason, with the pregnancy, it hurt too bad to do it like we used to. The pain was unbearable, and I tried, but we just couldn't go through with it.

"Aight, girl. Don't start nothing you can't finish," Caesar warned, getting hard in my hand.

I knew he wanted sex just as bad as I should have but there was something about my pregnancy that threw off my libido. However, that day I wanted to please him and just sitting there in that hot ass apartment, staring at him with his shirt off showing off all them damn tats and rippled muscles had me getting moist between my thighs.

"I can suck it… get some of that pressure off, if you like," I purred seductively with a grin.

He just gave me a subtlety glance but underneath the surface I saw his sex face hidden like the sun behind a sublime cloud.

I realized he was playing hard and I liked that, so I stroked him more, increasing in speed until he exhaled a sigh of air and leaned back on the couch. His face scrunched up into an expression that I'm certain he didn't know turned me, and all the ladies who'd ever seen it. He bit down on his lubricious bottom lip and arched his brow, looking at me just like the man everyone said he resembled: Trey Songz. Only he was sexier, with a mane of short cropped wavy hair, a handsomely trimmed beard with a mouth full of gold teeth. Normally, I didn't date guys with grills in their mouths, but I had to make an exception when it came to Caesar. He was just that sexy.

"Damn, you gettin' my dick hard as fuck, bae."

I was immediately turned on. Call me a vixen, but there was no better feeling then when a woman is in complete control of her man. It's like femininity conquering masculinity and there are perks that comes with that, especially when you're pregnant. I got so wet that I could have wrung my panties with both hands and they still wouldn't be dry.

He placed his large hand on the back of my neck and squeezed it. That was always a prelude to oral sex for him. I stilled his hand and looked up at him with a quid pro quo.

"After I do this, we goin' to Pappadeaux for crabs and shrimp, right?"

You could ask for anything from a man anticipating some head and, ten times out of ten, you would get it.

"You ain't shit," he quipped with a smirk as he continued to watch my hands manipulate his pants, massaging his dick like a masseuse.

I couldn't help but giggle. The weed smoke was still going up my nose. Where we were from, women smoked blunts throughout their pregnancy, so I didn't think nothing of getting it secondhand. I didn't know any better so I was enjoying the high. I stroked him faster, eliciting a groan and causing his hand to travel down and squeeze my thigh so hard that he left a print.

"Make that lobster, crabs *and* shrimps," he said with a smile.

He then reached over and pinched my nipple. I flinched. It was sore and swollen. It hurt.

"Ouch!"

"My bad, bae."

Softening his touch, he caressed my nipple between his forefinger and thumb like how you would put out a wooden match if it were on fire. Whatever the case, within seconds, he had me on hot. Regardless of the inconvenience of swollen, sore nipples I was really thinking about jumping on his dick. But just when I was about to pull out his manhood and please my man, my phone started to ring.

Damn!

I wanted to toss that bitch out the window but instead I anxiously peered at the number. I was waiting for financial aid to approve my grant and I prayed this was the call that I was waiting on, telling me that the money was headed to my bank account. Curious, Caesar looked at the number, too.

It damn sure wasn't financial aid.

"Shit," I cursed under my breath.

I made a mental note to have the number blocked, just as I had a million times before. When Caesar recognized the number, his body went rigid as he pulled away from me. I noticed his demeanor change. In mere seconds, he was toxic, like poisonous, dark clouds suddenly blocking a beautiful sun.

"Answer it!" he said in a clipped tone.

With his brows knotted up he looked at me with pure hostility.

"Do I have to? I can just let it ring and we can finish what we started. I can please you… do all the things you like me to do."

I was talking fast like words on a string, a monotone of pungent pleas, until Caesar interrupted me. He was like a volcano spewing lava as he erupted on me.

"Didn't I tell you to answer the muthafuckin' phone? Don't fuckin' play me. Tell that nigga not to call you no more. Tell him who I am, that we havin' a baby and you fuckin' gettin' married!" Caesar yelled, spraying my face with spittle. For the first time in my life, I actually feared he might hit me.

"Okay, okay…." I said out loud but, really, I was trying hard to bridle my nerves as I brushed the palms of my hands down on my thighs nervously, again the baby started kicking. This time it felt like he wanted to come out. I winced, sucking in sips of air like I was underwater breathing through a straw.

I answered the phone with a trembling hand with Caesar watching me intensely.

This was about to ruin our entire day.

What I didn't know was things were about to go terribly wrong, tragic.

Chapter Two

~
Sunday

"You have received a call from an inmate from a Federal facility. To accept this call, dial 9. To refuse, simply hang up."

A feminine mechanical voice spoke as I cradled the phone in my hand, staring at it as if it were a dead pigeon. I was horrified to the depths of my soul and one of the reasons was because, the man on the other end of the line, still had a grip on me I couldn't let go. The problem was that he was also the devil in flesh. He had hurt me to my core, and almost got me locked up for life. I was his lover, his soon to be wife at the time. After spending eight years of my life, who would have ever thought our love could have ended in ruins like this? He was currently on death row about to be executed for hideous crimes, that I was once nearly convicted of.

"Hello?"

"Sunday... I was just calling to tell you something," King said, his voice making my entire body go warm.

In the background, there was the cacophony of sounds, like human anguish, voices resonating in what sounded like the gallows of hell. Men, chained and fitted in cells, awaiting a fate that their destiny had already chosen: Death by lethal injection. They would spend idle time, awaiting their destiny in mental torment, waiting for the grim reaper to call their names.

"King… y-you can't call here anymore," I stammered in a high pitch tone.

My eyes began to water, and my entire body was shaking as Caesar watched me with his eyes hooded in contempt. King didn't say anything on the other line for a few moments as I held on the line. Our silence was a thief, stealing borrowed time from a dying man. Then, finally, King said something as Caesar continued glaring at me, his face beginning to crease into a formidable frown.

"Oh… I get it. If that's how you want it, it's cool," King replied.

"Tell that nigga why!" Caesar said loud enough for him to hear as he slid closer to me, invading my space.

"It's because… I'm pregnant. I'm about to have a baby and get married to my fiancé, Caesar."

I closed my eyes as a tear cascaded down my cheek then I quickly mopped at it with the back of my hand, hoping that Caesar didn't see it. No matter how much I denied it, King still had a hold on me.

A pregnant pause followed. I held my breath until King started speaking again.

"Oh… Listen, I'm happy for you and dude. I wish you nothing but the best. I was just calling to tell you that I was granted an appeal from the 11th circuit. They gon' give me a hearing concerning the DNA hair fiber. After that, I'm hoping to either get a new trial or they gon' have to set me free or rule against me again."

"What? Who? I mean, how? There were three bodies—that baby was murdered and they said that somebody possibly molested her." I was spilling my words out like I had diarrhea of the mouth. The baby kicked my ass like a horse and then stopped again when I pressed my hand to my stomach.

"I told you I wasn't guilty. I ain't do that shit and I'm sorry you got caught up in all the madness. I never wanted to hurt you. There isn't a day that goes by that I don't think about you and what happened. I only wanted to protect you, but somebody set me up—" King was saying before Caesar snatched the phone out my hand.

"Listen, my nigga, what she sayin' is you don't need to call here no muthafuckin mo'! She got a man!"

"So this must be Caesar," King began, chuckling a little after he said it. "You the little nigga that used to sell weed on the block, outside my trap. I'm sure you remember me and my legacy. Do me a favor. Don't get on the phone tryna impress Sunday and write a check yo' ass can't cash. I'm tryin' to respect you, bruh, 'cause, in reality, she's my old chick and I'ma be home soon. You need to let her tell me not to call. I don't need to hear that shit from you, bruh, if you know what I mean."

The entire time I looked on, appalled. King had never spoke to me in this tone, but I could easily pick up on his current temperament because I knew him best. He was furious but, like always, his voice was cool and calculated, like a grizzly bear walking on ice. When he got like this, he was lethal.

"Hey, tell this nigga I said don't call no fuckin' more!" Caesar ranted and threw the phone in my lap.

I picked it up with trembling hands. I could feel the baby moving around inside me, like he could sense there was something wrong. I tried to speak but it came out jumbled and jagged like I was lock-jawed, causing me to chew on my words until I finally managed to say what I intended. It was my heart speaking, not my mind. Deep in my heart, I knew I would always love King; I just wasn't in love with him anymore. Or at least, I didn't think I was.

"King, if you do get out, they gon' kill you. Don't come back here, don't call my phone, and don't contact me. Act like I never existed... like you never knew me. I never want to see you again, King, you hear me? You fucked it all up!"

I knew as soon as the words came out my mouth that I was being too emotional—too personal. I still harbored feelings, feelings that I wanted to bury in a tomb. Even then, my feelings for King were too deep to ignore.

I hung up the phone and began to sob uncontrollably as Caesar stood over me. There was no compassion in his heart, no empathy, no nothing for me when it came to King. The only thing he ever showed in regard to me and King was jealousy and rage. I knew that no matter what I said he could tell that I still loved King and probably always would. King and I had been together for over eight years; I'd suffered three miscarriages and a broken heart over him.

King had been with me since I was fifteen and he was seventeen. I was with him back when he was nothing but a small-time drug dealer and jack-boy. Then the day emerged, like a prickly thorn, when he grew through the ghetto concrete and became a ruthless drug lord and a notorious killer; hated by many but respected by all. King hit a big lick and robbed a Haitian gang in Miami, overseen by his own plug, and came up with 500 kilos of coke each valued in the streets at $24,000. With everything he needed to build his empire in his hands, King never looked back, and I was by his side.

Caesar knew of King even before I got with him. On more than one occasion, he had thrown up in my face during a fight about how he'd seen me riding with King in his convertible Bentley and other fancy cars, some that I couldn't even remember us being in. Even in King's absence he was still a part of my life, like an ugly scar that wouldn't go away.

On my right shoulder, near my breast plate, I had a big flaming tattoo embellished in pink and purple roses with the words, 'King & Sunday Forever' in the middle. Caesar hadn't noticed the tattoo until the very first time he made love to me. After he saw it, he had trouble getting an erection. He never told me why, but I already knew.

I tried to conceal the tattoo as much as I could and even made a promise to Caesar to one day have it removed but what I couldn't have removed was the indelible print he had left on my aching heart. That much was apparent from my conversations with him whenever he called.

"You still love him, don't you?" Caesar shouted over me.

"No, I love you! Please, don't start this again. Please, Caesar," I sobbed harder, wrapping my belly in my arms.

"I don't know what to think. And then there is this whole marriage thing; you're 'bout to be my wife. You're pregnant with my baby but it feels like you still got feelings for that other nigga. Maybe we need to rethink this thing." He began to pace across the floor.

I looked up through my tears, startled.

"Rethink what? I love you. I don't want to live without you, Caesar..."

With my arms spread wide, I reached out to him. He shook his head at me and I winced, not because of him but because the baby was stirring hard in my stomach. My abdomen got tight and I sucked in a sharp breath. I wasn't due for a month or so.

These must be Braxton-Hicks contractions... my body is just gettin' ready.

"If he does get out and come home, I feel like this is going to be in issue."

"You heard what I told him. I don't want to see him ever again, you heard me tell him that!"

"No, what I heard was you warn him not to come back here so he don't get killed. Then you went into all that shit 'bout not contactin' you which sounded generic as fuck to me."

I sucked in deep breath. His accusations were starting to annoy me, maybe because he was more right than wrong. I expelled a wary sigh as if trying to control my breathing and calm my mood as not to excite the baby. I couldn't remember the baby ever being so active before. It was like he was feeding off my emotions.

"We have too much invested in each other for you to feel like another man can take your place. I love—"

"Too much invested? I've only known you for barely two years. You was fuckin' that other nigga for nearly a decade and you still driving the Benz he gave you, wearing the jewelry he bought and let's not forget that big ass tattoo on your fuckin' breast with his name on it."

He was belligerent as he snatched at the shirt that I was wearing in an attempt to expose the tattoo. I swatted his hand, clawing at it with my long fingernails, nearly drawing blood. The moment had become volatile that fast.

"Hold up, nigga, you really in your feelings? First of all, what am I supposed to do, give away an expensive car and jewelry that was given to me? It's not his shit, it's mine!"

Caesar opened his mouth to speak but I cut his ass off.

"I'm not done! As for the tattoo, I already told you that I was goin' to get it taken off, but now I don't have the time or the money for it. And the jewelry he gave me, is just that: Something that was *given* to me. It's old."

"Yeah, right. You gon' keep that ugly ass shit tatted on you forever. Stop lying!" he spat back, raising his fist like he was about to hit me.

That was it! I was on my feet with the quickness, ready to fight his ass if it came to it. I wasn't one to let a man put his hands on me.

"*Ugly*?" I frowned, shouting in his face. "Ugly? It wasn't ugly when you was fuckin' me, kissing all over it. And I know you not givin' me shit 'bout the same car that you love to drive. Don't try to belittle me over some simple shit because you jealous of King."

Caesar's frown deepened but I could tell that I'd really hit a nerve. Behind his steel glare was a hint of shock and embarrassment, as if I had knowledge of something he was embarrassed to admit.

"Why would I be jealous of him? Like really, this nigga locked up! And if he do come home, these niggas on the block gon' kill him for what he did to that little girl. Them John Doe Boys done fell off, so they can't do shit. That said, tell me why the fuck should I be jealous of a dead man?"

The John Doe Boys that Caesar was referring to was King's crew, and we both knew that he was lying. Even in King's absence over the years, they hadn't lost a step. They weren't as ruthless with killing, but still they ruled the city with an iron fist, with the help of King's ex, conniving ass Makita, who couldn't stand me. I had taken him from her way back in high school. She was just as gangsta as any man and that may have been what attracted King to me. Caesar knew of both of them and he knew how well Makita was running things. It was becoming more apparent from his ravings that he was hating hard.

"Fuck you, Caesar! You literally make me fuckin' sick. Maybe we do need to rethink this marriage thing," I fumed, crossing my arms across my chest.

Just then, Kirk, Caesar's brother, walked into the room with his friend, Saz, stalking behind him. He had a slice of pizza in his hand and a can of Coke. He wore cutoff jeans and a Black Panther t-shirt along with matching flip-flops and socks. Saz sported an Avenger's shirt, munching on a slice of pizza like he hadn't eaten in years.

Though he was a few years younger than Kirk, mentally, they were on the same level.

"Y'all want some pizza? It's fresh out the oven. I got drinks, too. I made eighty bucks at the car wash today with my boy, Saz."

Beside him, Saz continued chewing and wagged his head. "Yeah, me too. It was a good day for tips."

I shot Saz a pointed look. He may have made some money today, but we all knew it wasn't from working at no car wash. Saz was an up and coming corner boy who peddled a few dime and nickel bags for a few dollars every now and then.

"No to the pizza. We good," Caesar said and waved him off.

Kirk gave me a sympathetic glance. I could tell he knew that we had been arguing and this was his way of defusing the situation. Even though he wasn't that smart, when it came to human kindness, he was a sweetheart, like a gentle giant.

"I'll take a slice, Kirk," I said just to piss Caesar off. Plus, I was a little hungry, too. I knew, like always, he just wanted to rush his brother off. Caesar wanted nothing more than to continue to vent his frustrations out on me.

Kirk plodded over and gave me his slice of pizza on a napkin along with the unopened can of Coke. Watching him, Caesar was seething.

"Kirk, can ya'll get da fuck out? I need to talk to her!"

He turned around and crinkled his brow at his little brother. "Hold up, man. You ain't just gonna talk to me any kinda way, bruh."

Kirk was slow in the thinking department at times, but he wasn't no push over.

"Ok, I'ma say it nicely. Get da fuck out!" Caesar snapped.

Kirk scowled at his brother with a look of indignation and took several steps toward him, angrily raising his hand in the air.

Suddenly, there was a knock at the door. At that moment, both brothers ignored it, glaring at each other as Saz and I looked on anxiously. The knock came again, and Caesar tore his eyes away from Kirk before stomping over to the door and snatching it open. In his haste, he neglected to look through the peephole—a tragic mistake because, immediately, all hell broke loose.

My eyes filled with horror when I saw three masked gunmen storm in with assault rifles and handguns clutched in the fists of their outstretched hands.

"Nobody fuckin' move!"

Foolishly, Saz instantly went for the gun he had stashed at his waist.

Big mistake.

KA-BOOM!

He was shot at close range right toward his chest. The impact from the gun sent him propelling backwards.

An earth-shattering scream pierced my ears as chaos ensued all around me. It wasn't until I felt pain gripping my chest, my body fighting for oxygen to fill my empty lungs, that I realized the scream had come from me.

Chapter Three

~ Sunday

My ears rang like someone had shot a cannon close to my head as a splash of incandescent white light exploded in my brain.

All the masked gunmen stormed in on us. They were moving fast as my world suddenly started to strobe on the precipice of disaster.

This can't be happening.

"Where is the dope and money at?" one of the gunmen shouted. He was short and stubby, built like a tank, and dressed like one too, wearing an army fatigue jacket, blue jeans and boots.

"No, no! Saz, get up!" Kirk shouted at him; he was frantic. I feared the worse. Kirk was unpredictable when he got caught up in his emotions. I had no idea what he would do.

One of the gunmen warned him. "Big man, shut the fuck up!"

"Y'all just shot my friend! Get up, Saz! Get up!" Kirk moved like he was about to go over and help him up as Saz wailed loudly in pain. He was alive but badly injured, from the deep red blood that was covering his chest.

One of the gunmen rushed over and violently struck Kirk upside the head with the butt of an assault rifle, opening up a deep gash that immediately started spewing blood. I dropped the can of Coke to the floor in shock and Caesar started to run to my side, only to be greeted by a pistol to the chest from one of them men.

"Bitch, where the muthafuckin' money at?" another gunman said and placed a .9mm to my head. Through his mask I could see his diamond grill. His fetid breath was hot on my face and his bloodshot red eyes looked maniacal.

Unable to hold my bladder, I pissed down my leg onto the carpet. I had never been so frightened in my entire life.

"There is money and more drugs in the bedroom," I said as my entire body shook.

In the next instance, I was nearly yanked off my feet by my hair as the shorter gunman rushed over and grabbed me, shoving me harshly toward the bedroom. The entire time I could hear Saz moaning in agony.

Then there was Caesar's voice.

"No, Sunday!"

Boom!

From the sound of metal against bone, someone had delivered him a blow to the head. I swallowed hard, walking faster as I lead the gunman to our bedroom to show him Caesar's stash. It was in the back of my closet, in a shoe box, buried under other boxes, clothes and miscellaneous items. There was probably a total of nineteen-thousand dollars inside. Caesar had cut out a section of the wall and made a make-shift door for his self-made safe. There was about twenty pounds of loud along with the money, our total life savings.

"It's there," I said, pointing to the door that led to the safe. The first gunman motioned to another man beside him who went to check. After he pulled out the contents inside, the first gunman turned back to me.

"Lie across the bed. Face down. Hurry!"

I closed my eyes and did as ordered, praying just like my Mama had taught me to in times of need, same as her mother taught her.

"Yea, thou I walk through the valley of the shadows of death, I will fear no evil. For thou are with me…"

My eyes pinched tight when I felt a pistol pressed at the back of my skull. My heart was pounding in my chest like an African drum.

"We got the money and his stash. Nigga, we hit the lottery! Let's finish them off so we can be out."

I prayed harder. "Your rod and your staff, they comfort me…"

Then things went from bad to worse. I heard Kirk growl and then there was a loud crashing nose, a huge thump against the wall and the entire apartment shook like an earthquake and a seismic boom! There was another tumultuous crash. I could hear what sounded like tables and chairs being overturned, bodies being flung, men yelling.

I was *terrified*.

"Thou preparest a table for me in the presence of my enemies. Thou anoints my head with oil. My cup runneth over…" I continued to pray as all hell erupted around me.

The struggle in the next room continued. I hoped that my prayers were going from my lips to God's ears and Kirk was able to save us. Unlike Caesar, who was muscular, but much smaller in comparison, Kirk was nearly seven feet and almost three hundred pounds. He was massive and could be a problem; he had crazy, brute strength.

Suddenly, I heard one of the gunmen cry out in panic.

"Shit, man! He took my gun!"

I felt a ray of hope. God was in the prayer-answering business.

"Surely, goodness and mercy shall follow me all the days of my life…

BOOM! BOOM! BOOM!

Shots rang out and I heard a body drop. I screamed, clutching on to the bed sheets for dear life. My heart was beating madly, and my baby started to stir. As I held my breath, time seemed to stall like infinity. Forever waiting…

Then, I heard one of the gunmen start to speak.

"What? I *had* to shoot him. His big ass took that gun and then slung ol' boy out there like a fuckin rag doll."

My heart sank like a ship with a giant hole in the bottom.

The man then added, "You good in there, Daze?"

"Nigga, da fuck you callin' my gotdamn name for? You stupid ass, muthafucka!" I heard the gunman in the room with me say. Horror seized my entire body.

I knew the name. Daze was street dude, a rival that had been warring with the John Doe Boys for years back before King got locked up. In fact, King had killed one of Daze's men in the parking lot near the strip club, Magic City. They had a heated argument inside that spilled out onto the streets. Eventually guns were drawn, and King prevailed.

My breath caught in my lungs when I heard the sound of footfalls coming back down the hall toward me.

"Lord help me, *please*…" I continued to pray.

"Man, my bad. That big ass nigga tried us. I had to put a cap in his head, slump his ass. I shot Caesar too. He still alive, but not for long from the way that nigga leakin.'"

"Shut up, nigga, so we can get da fuck outta here. Go put this in the duffle-bag."

I listened intently to the exchange.

The second man asked Daze, "And what you finna do?"

When I heard his reply, it made chills crawl down my spine.

"I'm finna have some fun with her. She's King's old bitch."

"But ain't she pregnant?" the first guy retorted. Daze made a grunting sound as if to say he didn't care either way.

I tried to rise. "No, please no!" I protested and was violently shoved back down.

"Fuck outta here, man! Go tie both them other niggas up. I'll be out in a minute, you stupid muthafucka!" Daze said.

I heard the sound of feet walking away and I began to resist again when Daze touched me. My heart beat fast in my chest. I felt his hand nudge at the boxer shorts that I was wearing. Beneath them, my panties were soaking wet. I had peed on myself earlier.

Unmoved by that, Daze began to pull and tug on my panties, trying to get them down. I continued to squirm.

"No, please don't," I objected and grabbed at his hand.

WHAM!

He struck me in the jaw with his fist so hard that I felt it crack. My head snapped back and all I saw were white spots and stars. Instantly, blood spewed from my mouth. There was so much, I nearly choked on it.

"Bitch, shut da fuck up! See what the fuck you made me do? I ruined my shoes with all yo' fuckin' blood drippin' on me." He scoffed evilly like the devil. I was dazed, disorientated and riveting with pain.

Daze tore my clothes off and I closed my eyes and beginning again to pray to God that He would have mercy on my soul and protect my unborn baby. I began to lose consciousness, willing it in order to block out the madness. I would always remember the hurt, the pain and I would never forget his name.

Daze.

Once he finished his assault, I was ushered out the room at gunpoint still naked from the waist down. So much blood continued to spew from my mouth which was aching to the point that I wondered if I should welcome death as a gift. I didn't know it, but my jaw was broken in two places.

What kind of animals would do this?

I would never forget the expression on Caesar's face when he looked up from the carpet and saw me. There was a puddle of blood, sanguine red all around him. He had been tied with his hands behind his back, lying face down on the carpet. Next to him was Kirk; he had a hole in his face the size of a fist. The entire back of his head was blown off, leaving only matter and gory brains and blood sprayed across the room and walls. It looked like an animal had been slaughtered. On his other side was Saz who, remarkably, was still alive, gasping his breaths and groaning from the pain of his gunshot womb.

There was so much blood.

"Sunday?"

Caesar called my name in a way that I had never heard him say it before. His voice echoed with melancholy as if we were both in a dream state—no—a horrific nightmare. He looked at me with his sorrows showing in his eyes.

"Caesar, I'm so sorry..." I began sob.

"Shut the fuck up!" one of the gunmen, that I hadn't noticed before, barked.

I was forced to my knees as the rancid stench of blood and death rushed through my nostrils. The baby started kicking wildly again and the pain was unbearable. It made me double over, wincing in agony.

"Oh God, it hurts!" I cried out, grabbing my stomach.

At the time, I didn't know I was having contractions and about to go into labor.

What really let me know my life was doomed was when I looked over at the gunman who had shouted at me and saw that he had his mask off. He was light-skinned and a thick beard with green eyes enclosed by long lashes like a girl. In my heart, I knew there was no way they were going to let me live after seeing their faces.

"What you got your mask off for?" Daze asked him.

"The big ass nigga pulled it off when he took my gun. That nigga was strong as a muthafucka, too."

"Damn right! Damn near broke my arm when he threw us across the room," the other gunman chimed in as he rubbed his arm.

"Tie this bitch up, pour gas on 'em all and shoot them. Then we need to roll out," Daze gave orders that forged a lump in my throat.

I gasped and turned to Caesar who was going in and out of consciousness. He was in bad condition, lying in a puddle of blood. From the loo of it, he wasn't going to make it. He was dying.

Neither am I, I thought, devastated.

"I left the gasoline in the van," the guy with the mask off said, gesturing with his hands.

"Fuck you mean 'you left it'? I handed it to you and told you to bring it!" Daze shot back.

"Yeah, nigga, but I was already carryin' the duffle bag, the shotgun and two pistols," he retorted.

To my surprise, the two began to argue back and forth as the other guy looked on incredulously. Neither of them was paying us any attention.

"Fuck it! Just shoot 'em in the head so we can bail outta here," Daze commanded.

"Noooo, please, don't," I began to plead and beg for my life. "I won't tell anyone. I promise, I swear to God—"

Before I could finish my sentence, I was violently slung to the floor. Luckily, I was able to use my hand to partially save my fall, but I still came down on my stomach. Excruciating pain racked my body and, just then, with strength I didn't know Caesar had, he rose from the floor, on one knee, wobbly and managed to push the guy nearest to him.

"Fuck you slam her on the floor for?" he shouted as blood spewed from his chest. His eyes flickered with terror and strength.

The gunman hit him with the butt of his .9mm, pistol-whipping him mercifully. I saw a tooth carom across the carpet as Caesar fell down, balling up into a fetal position, using his arms to ward off the blows.

"Y'all need to leave us the fuck alone!" Saz suddenly said as he awoke with deep cut spewing bleed from the side of his forehead.

He furtively reached toward his side where his gun was stashed. Before he was able to get it, Daze snatched him by the collar and took out a large bowing hunting knife. My eyes widened as I watched him move with quick precision and slice Saz's neck from ear-to-ear. Blood squirted nearly two feet high from his neck and sprayed the room.

I screamed to the top of my lungs clutching my chest. Caesar's entire face was wet with Saz's blood and it looked like he was going into shock from the sight of the young boy being killed right before his eyes. Saz's body shivered in convulsions as I screamed out for dear life.

Then he suddenly stopped moving.

He was dead.

"Tie the other two up, shoot 'em and let's get the fuck outta here. Like I fuckin' said before, we moving too slow!" Daze ordered again like he was frustrated and in a hurry. One of the gunmen moved quickly, securing all of our wrists with zip-ties, even Kirk's, though I knew he was dead.

"But… Daze, she pregnant," the green-eyed man said tentatively.

"Ion give a fuck! You shoot them or I'm shooting yo' ass. You walkin' round here without yo' mask on, fuck you think they gon' say if the police come?"

That was enough to convince him.

BLOCKA!

He shot Kirk, just to make sure he was dead, and then the other gunmen walked over to Caesar as the green-eyed one came toward me with his gun in his hands. I couldn't look at him. I closed my eyes and began to pray for my son.

"Man… Do I gotta do it? I mean, man, she *pregnant*. Can't you just slit her neck like you did the other one? I really don't—"

"Dumb ass, nigga, that is worse! How 'bout I slit yo' fuckin' throat? Now kill them and meet us outside. You know what King wanted us to do and I know you don't want it gettin' back to him that you ain't follow his orders. Make sure that gay ass nigga over there gets to watch you do it before you bust a cap in his ass, too."

The guy didn't respond. I looked up at him and saw that his hands were trembling. In his eyes, I could tell that he didn't want to harm me, but he was stuck battling between his duty and his morality.

"Nooo," I heard Caesar yell as his arms flailed.

The gunman walked over, aimed the gun at him and fired. Instantly, Caesar went limp as the bullet struck him in the chest. Next, he walked over and stood over me. That was when we both heard a police siren. I saw him flinch and slightly turn.

"Please don't kill me. My baby, I'm pregnant," I pleaded.

"Shut up! I gotta do this," he said, but I could tell his heart really wasn't into it as he held the gun over me. The barrel looked like the size of a cannon as I looked up and then saw him sneer at me like he finally had the guts to pull the trigger.

All I could do then was close my eyes like my mama had taught me and pray some more.

"Lord, I will fear no evil for thou art with me. Thy rod and thy staff, they comfort me..."

BLOCKA!

Chapter Four
~
King

Florence Federal Correctional Penitentiary, Supermax.
Death Row

I worked out in silence doing push-ups on the concrete cell floor as my anxiety got the best of me. Normally, I would do a thousand but this day I did double. With nothing else on my hands, all I had was time.

I had been away for nearly three years in prison and, after countless appeals being turned down, finally, I had a victory. An appellate court judge had ruled in my favor. It was a partial ruling, but it was hope, which was better than what I had. At the time, I was serving a sentence of death plus forty years for a triple homicide, a crime I had not committed. Truth be told, murder charges were most always picked up by the state the crimes were committed in, but because I was said to be the ringleader of one of the biggest organizations in the United States, The John Doe Boys, the Federal Government picked up my state case and charged me with the RICO Act, the Racketeering Influence and Corrupt Organizations Act, a federal law designed to combat organized crime.

To date, there were over 30,000 members of The John Doe Boys, not even counting in other states due to social media. The organization grew to astronomical numbers in the millions. There is power in numbers, so I became America's threat.

To make matters worse, I was serving out my sentence in a supermax facility on death row. This was America's most infamous and secure prison. You don't get to be a prisoner at ADX-Florence Colorado without having a measure of incredible violence in your case. Name a convicted terrorist, a foreign or domestic killer or a convicted organized gang leader and there is a strong likelihood they are right with me, serving eons of time without the possibility of parole in a eleven by nine feet box also known as a cell.

Larry Hoover, Terry Nicols, Ramzi Yousef, and Eric Rudolph are just a few high-profile felons who ended up here to do their time. In my opinion, they were lucky. At least they were sentenced with time. My sentence carried death.

I was sent straight to the D-wing, death row. I lived out my life on borrowed time. I was sort of a celebrity on the row. The good thing was, I would receive tons of mail from all over the United States. The prison had to have someone just to read through all the thousands of letters I would receive. My status as a very rich and powerful gang leader infuriated the guards, plus there was the fact that my crew were suspected for the murders of police officers who had killed innocent black men and women in cold blood for something simple as a routine traffic stop.

My two hood orphans, Bulletproof and Dolo, who I'd raised since they were around seven years old, were working to get me back on the streets. Both of their moms were addicted to drugs and they actually lived in the streets, homeless, at that age. Though I'd tried to get them in school, their moms and other family continued to call them back in the streets with their lifestyle so, eventually, I had to accept them for what they were: a product of their environment.

Between the two of them, with me as a mentor, they managed to organize the hood in a way that had never been done and brought a lot of young brothers and sisters in the hood together in unity. They rallied them under one common goal by starting businesses like Hit Records Entertainment, a very successful record label and several restaurants and nightclubs. They were also into real estate; they had bought up a lot of the eyesore abandoned homes in the neighborhood, remodeled them, and then sold them.

The only sore spot was when a white cop brutalized a pregnant black woman over an illegal traffic stop. She refused to get out of her car because she felt the stop was illegal and didn't warrant her to be searched. She was six months pregnant and the video went viral of the cop body-slamming her and kicking her in the face. In the end, the cop was found not guilty. Days later, the officer was discovered murdered in his patrol car with a note attached to his forehead that read:

Every time you harm one of ours, we killing one of yours. It was signed: JDB

There were also more instances where it was alleged that The John Doe Boys were suspected in killings in retaliation of other injustices, the violence of police brutality.

***

I was locked up twenty-three hours out of the day in an iron box with no human contact. The rule was that inmates couldn't communicate with each other and that went for the outside world, too. On the daily, I fought to keep my sanity like a championship boxer. Each day was a new round.

With a population of less than one percent of blacks working at the prison, it was a cesspool for racist white men with a personal agenda against black men like myself. I had been in physical altercations on more than one occasion but because I kept in shape, I managed to protect myself. However, there was one time when I nearly got my ass whooped.

The correctional officers tried to jump on me when I was being escorted to the recreation part of the prison while I was being handcuffed. A C.O. stole on me and I managed to break his jaw, but they did end up roughing me up pretty bad. It's amazing what you can do with a head-butt and other perfectly timed maneuvers designed for self-defense.

Last one hundred, King. Let's go. Keep ya mind right. It's almost time for you to be done with this shit.

Once again, for what seemed like the umpteenth time, I thought about what had happened to bring me to this point. I had been convicted of four grisly, tragic homicides. One of the victims was a four-year-old girl. Two confidential informants testified against me, sealing my fate. One of them was my sister's boyfriend, Andre Forte. It was a complete lie; however, it did earn him a reduced sentence for a drug charge.

As for my sister, Nikki, l loved her and supported her even after her man Andre turned snitch and agreed to testify against me in return for a lighter sentence. At the time, he was facing a drug and weapon charge, carrying a forty-year sentence. After his testimony where he lied and said he saw me coming out the victim's apartment on the morning of the triple homicide killings, he was released, and I found out later the Feds had paid him $50,000 for his testimony against me.

There were three other guys currently serving life sentences with me because of Andre jumping on their cases with his lies. I had made a solemn oath if I ever got out of prison, off death row, I was going to kill him, but Bulletproof and Dolo got to him before I had the chance. I was sure that Nikki had to know by now that my team was behind his murder. I couldn't help but wonder if she would forgive me.

Even with all of the things that happened, the worse of all was that my ex-fiancée, Sunday Kennedy, the love of my life, had got caught up in all the madness. I had sent her to pick up some money from one of my homies and when she got there, strangely, the front door was open.

According to her, when she walked in, the place was a shamble with overthrown chairs, furniture askew. It was in the living room that she discovered the bodies. Tony Span and his girl, Renee, were regular people in their 30s, high school sweethearts with a four-year-old child, Aaliyah. She was adorable and she was also my goddaughter. Just like her parents, she had been shot in the head and bound by duct tape, with her throat slashed.

The moment I got the call from Sunday, I was in Colombia, the cocaine capital of the world, parlaying a shipment of coke so big that we had to weigh it all on a scale you normally use for whales. I had scored over a hundred million dollars' worth of product with the connect, Santiago, who claimed to be a relative of Pablo Escobar's grandson. I was illegally in the country with a fake passport and I.D.; there was nothing I could do when I got the call from Sunday but instruct her to get the money and get the fuck out of there!

I'll never forget that day. It was like yesterday when Sunday called with the devastating news. I tried to do everything in my power to keep her calm, even though I wasn't. Tony Span and his family were like my own family, like blood. We grew up together, stayed in the same building in the 4th Ward of Atlanta but Tony never ran the streets, sold drugs or got into trouble. He was a good athlete, had a scholarship to play football. He hurt his leg a week after finding out that Renee was pregnant with the baby and dropped out of school to find a job. I was moving major weight by then, so I paid him two grand a month to allow me to stash money at his house. He was the only one I could trust other than my sister and my mom.

I had about seven mill stashed various places in his house, split and buried in different places. I'd asked Sunday to grab about fifty grand of it that day. After discovering the bodies, she began scrambling around the house, crying hysterically as she searched all of the stash spots. She found the first stash and was making her way to the second, when the police pulled up. She was trying to stuff as much as she could in the pillowcase and get away when they charged in and arrested her for three homicides and robbery.

I had almost completed my push-ups and was sweating pretty good when the high-tech motion door slid opened. It led to another door, made of cast-iron steel with a slate to pass food or mail though. It also served as a porthole to peer inside the cell and, on a few occasions, tear gas had been thrown in on me when I refused to come out in order to have my cell searched.

"Listen, my nigga, what she sayin' is you don't need to call here no-muthafuckin-mo'. She got a man!"

I chuckled derisively to myself, thinking about the fake ass thug that Sunday called herself dealing with at the moment. In my mind, he was just keeping her company. There hadn't been a single day that went by and I didn't think of her and, as soon as I got out of my current predicament, my goal was to make her mine again. I just hoped she would forgive me for almost destroying her life.

As Sunday was getting arrested for robbery and a triple-homicide, I was on a little ass landing strip, the size of a football field, in Narino, the far southwest side of Antioquia, hidden in a rural area in the tall dense jungles of Colombia. They had mosquitoes the size of butterflies, along with large man-eating poisonous snakes, jaguars and other dangerous wild animals but come to find out that wasn't the only real danger.

As we loaded bales of coke, we were ambushed by gorillas dressed in army fatigue. My immediate suspicion was that they were Santiago goons. Being a hood nigga, I was prepared for it. After being born and raised in the rough streets of Atlanta, I already peeped this as one of the oldest tricks in the book. Sell the vic some dope, then rob them later and take it back. It was an easy come-up; you would have the product and the money.

They had a nice plan, but the wrong nigga.

There was a shoot-out and two of my homies, childhood friends, were murdered right before my eyes. I blamed myself for their deaths because I'd been distracted. My mind was on Sunday. The last thing I'd heard before she ended the call was her screaming that the police were coming. I was worried about her and couldn't do a damn thing about it.

Miraculously, a few members of my team and I were able to make it out, but only after a fierce gun battle. We flew back into the States on a small ass plane that was specially built to travel long distances but still small enough to not be detected by radar if we flew low at the right height. I made it safely back, but I still had one huge problem: Sunday. I needed to free her, but the problem was, I had no viable alibi at the time. I couldn't tell them the truth and, even if I did, no one would believe me but the other men who had been there with me, three men who were now free and very rich. My logic was I'd just wing it since I hadn't done the crime.

With no other options, I took the charge for Sunday and confessed that I knew about the money only. The prosecutor eagerly accepted my confession because of my reputation in the streets. Once he had me, I was charged with three counts of homicide, money laundering, conspiracy to traffic drugs and just about anything else they could throw at me. The mere fact I didn't have an alibi was one of the nails in the coffin. With the lack of evidence, I didn't think it made that much of a difference, but the jury did.

The only piece of substantial evidence was a strand of hair found on my goddaughter's pants, DNA evidence that had been tested and come back inconclusive as to whether it belonged to me. For that reason, I began to file appeals and now, I finally had a chance.

"Inmate Banks, time to get dressed. You got a court appearance," the C.O. yelled.

I looked up through the sweat burning my eyes. They were four-deep, dressed in riot gear, shields and other archaic ancient looking prison garb, along with weapons that they were prepared to whoop my ass with, if I let them.

It didn't bother me because I was more than ready to go. I was on my feet with the quickness, a sheen of perspiration gleaming off my chest and arms as I strolled over to the doors.

"No working out in the cell. I should write you up!" one of the dumb ass officers said.

I had a feeling it was the officer by the name of Smitty. He was a short rotund man with a ring of dirty, stringy blond hair and a bald plate in the middle of his head that resembled a bird's nest on his big ass head.

"Write up these nuts! Fuck you mean? I got handed all this fuckin' time and y'all always on a nigga 'bout workin' out in this little ass torture box," I said.

"Watch your fucking mouth!" came the response. One of them kicked on the heavy steel, cell door.

"Watch yo' fuckin' mouth, with yo' redneck ass!" I mouthed back, as I bounced over to the door and peered out.

Just like I knew. It was Smitty's old, evil, potbelly ass, with bloodshot red eyes makin' him look like a basset hound gone wild. I was full of testosterone and anger. Our relationship was pure combative and hostile like the gang wars that existed in the prison system.

"We should let yo' black ass stay in there and miss court," another C.O. threatened.

I couldn't help but chuckle at that mockingly. Prisons are run by a bureaucratic hierarchy with the federal judge at the top of the structure. The C.O. is at the opposite end of the totem pole and most of them hate their job, they get paid the least and do the most, they are only one tier higher than the convicts, so, basically, in the grand scheme of things they take out their anger on convicts.

"Smitty, fuck you, man! We both know that if you all don't take me to court, they gone lock you ole ass up and you going to be in a cell with Booty Bandit playing spades for ass. Get da fuck outta here, white boy!"

I almost laughed at the expression on his suddenly pale face as he knocked on the door with the baton that he wasn't even supposed to be carrying.

I listened as they stood in the hall, pretending to be occupied leaving me alone with my thoughts. I walked over and laid on my bunk, nonchalant like I wasn't more excited than I had ever been in my entire life. This was my last hope, I just needed to keep my composure and hope for the best. Finally, they opened my cell door to get me and it was one of the biggest reliefs of my life, however, I was apprehensive too. In life, there is always the fear of failure that lurks in your mind whenever you take on a challenge.

This was a *huge* challenge.

****

It had been a minute since I had on civilian clothes. I was wearing some baggy blue jeans, a gray t-shirt, and some off-brand gym shoes that were three sizes too big. The tags on the clothes said Walmart, but I didn't care. They were better than prison clothes and smelled better too. I was happy as hell to have them on! In the past, I wouldn't get caught dead in a get-up like this, but my only concern was getting out of the cold, inhumane prison cell where I would have languished 24/7. That day, I was anxious to see the sunshine.

The only downside was that I was still wearing jewelry, courtesy of the Federal Government D.O.C. The chains holding me down were heavy as shit as I waited to be escorted out the supermax facility. They had me wrapped up like I was a danger to society and a platoon of guards stood around, the security was heavy. Everyone was on notice that King Banks was finally about to leave the building.

I wasn't even prepared for what would happen next.

Chapter Five

~ King ~

I was airlifted on a shitty government plane that had seen better days. We traveled to Atlanta, to the U.S. Court of Appeals for the Eleventh Circuit. As soon as we landed at the airport, I was shoved into a van, surrounded by a caravan of cars. You would have thought I was a big cartel drug dealer. Technically speaking I was, but this shit was ridiculous. We drove with a car in front of me and another in the back. I sat in the middle vehicle wedged between two marshals that barely talked to me. Riding in silence, looking out the window, I placed my thoughts on the bright, majestic sun which I imagined was beckoning me to freedom.

There's a chance I can go home, I thought. I could barely believe it.

It had been a long time since I had seen the sun and the streets. Downtown Atlanta was bubbling with people and beautiful black women but at the moment, I could only think of one. Well, two, but after the way that Sunday put her nigga on the phone when I called her, my attitude was 'fuck both of 'em'. I was entitled to a free phone call once I made it to my destination and I planned on calling my ex.

Though we hadn't been together in a while, Makita had been holding me down since I got locked up and had quickly moved from being a player on the bench to a star component in my life. There was actually a chance for a future together for us. Her loyalty to me had been nothing short of God sent. She was the glue that kept my operations working while I was on death row fighting for my life. I'd always been told 'if you want to find out who your real friends are, go to prison'. When I got locked up, a lot of people who I thought would stick around left me hanging, but Makita never did that. Now I was about to have a chance to be free and I would remember the ones who stayed by my side; Makita being the main one.

****

Just as I suspected, the Feds had a plan for me. I was driven to the Atlanta Federal Penitentiary and placed in a segregation cell, sequestered from all the other convicts, not even given a phone call or a window to look out of. A convict, named Keith, worked as an orderly and he was the only one I was able to connect with once I got there.

"Aye, they don't give nobody no calls down here?" I asked him, catching his attention when I saw him come forward with a broom in hand.

"Nah, you might have to call your lawyer for that. They be trippin' up in here. Especially when it comes to niggas like you, head of The JDB."

As soon as he mentioned my crew, I tensed up wondering whether to consider him a friend or foe. He lifted his hands up, instantly seeing the alarm in my eyes.

"Listen, man, I got nothing but respect for you and your crew. My brother ran a trap and The JDBs used to serve him weight. What he made from that put food on my mama's table. You got a loyal friend right here." He jabbed his thumb to his chest. "Matter of fact, I take out the trash in the visitor's bathroom," he added, dropping his voice barely above a whisper. "If you get a visitor with something special in hand for you... they should make sure to use it."

I caught what he was saying and gave him a simple nod. Makita would definitely be down to smuggle some weed, a phone or anything else into the jail for me if I asked. The only problem was, I had no idea when I would be granted a visit. So far, things weren't looking too good.

It wasn't until day, just when I was about to start wrecking some shit, that I finally had a visitor come through. My lawyer, Dick Masson, was one of the best criminal defense lawyers in the state. He was an older man in his sixties and expensive as hell. He was thin with gray hair that sprouted at the sides and top with eyes that were deep-socketed and blue. His face was pleasant with a jutting chin that reminded me of Abraham Lincoln with the beard to match. As usual, he was dressed immaculate in a gray two piece with a burgundy tie that matched his shoes.

I was handcuffed to a steel rod in the room two tiers down from my cell and the sound of inmates resonated around us echoing so loud I had to raise my voice so he could hear me speak.

After greeting me with a quick pump of my hand, he took his seat.

"The hearing will be tomorrow. Sorry for the inconvenience but this is how the government works with high profile cases like yours," he explained. "They don't move fast."

That's a fuckin' understatement, I thought.

"And they don't give you the best accommodations..." Gesturing with his arms spread, he commented on the squalor of the small room we were in, located right next to the officers' station so they could keep a close eye on us. "You'll be separated from everyone else until your court date."

I nodded my head as I tried not to listen to the various sounds around us

"Great, I just want to get this over because, under the law, if they throw out the evidence of the hair and fiber, then the murder convictions and the conspiracy charges and others have to be thrown out, too. Right?" I asked, leaning forward. When I shifted, the chains rattled on my ankles and wrists.

Masson glanced down at my legs and frowned.

"You're right, and I like our chances. This case shouldn't have never made it to this point, but I will say, your reputation in the streets is what really hurt you. The government still feels you're running a gang. The John Doe Boys are a real threat and not just to Atlanta to America. After The JDB music production company was started, the members grew exponentially, and it's started an entire movement across the nation. You have a lot of supporters, even celebrities. There are threats of riots and violence if you're not let go. And, as you know, the Federal government doesn't negotiate with terrorists."

My brows jumped. "Terrorists?"

"Yes, The JDB gang is being referred to as domestic terrorists," he said as he dove through some papers in his briefcase. And added, "Last month during a traffic stop, a twenty-year-old black man was accidently shot and killed in front of his wife and two daughters when the police said they mistake his driver's license for a gun. Three weeks later, that cop was murdered in a Kroger's parking lot, he was with his wife and family. A note was left on his car, signed by The JDB, that said, '*Every time you murder one of ours, we killing one of yours*'. This has to stop, that cop was with his children."

"What about the black brotha that was killed in front of his children. That don't matter?"

"That was an accident. The officer that was killed in the store was a law-abiding citizen," my attorney responded.

"Shit, we live in two different worlds. In my world, white cops kill innocent black men almost daily."

"Not as much as black people kill each other," he responded.

"That makes it justified?" I asked as I looked at my attorney. He was starting to irk me. All I could do was mop my face with the palm of my hand as he shook his head at me like I didn't get it.

"Even while you have been in prison, the government still feels like you're running an illegal drug empire and you're still a serious threat."

"Fuck that! This America. It ain't a crime to be in a gang until you get caught up. It ain't right for me to be judged for something I ain't even been convicted of. John Doe Boys and whatever else."

"You're right but juries have been known to find a defendant guilty based off that, even though it's not supposed to be considered. Then there is the testimony of the people that testified against you," he added.

"Fuckin' rats. They were lyin' and shit to get a time cut. I wonder what they gon' do if I beat this case."

I sighed deeply and glanced up at the celling as he slid a sheaf of papers at me.

"What's that?" I asked.

"Case law. Read it and remember it. It's pertaining to your hearing. Hopefully, you can walk out of here a free man tomorrow or at least get a new hearing."

I couldn't help but smile for the first time in what felt like years. Then a thought crossed my mind.

"A friend of mine, Makita, and my mom was on my visitation list when I was at the pen in Colorado. Can I call them and get visits?" I asked with suddenly with enthusiasm from the probability of seeing a familiar face.

My lawyer furrowed his brow.

"I remember Ms. Makita. She was pretty," he said with a with a hint of a smile as the corners of his mouth turned up, he then crossed his legs.

I cut a glance at his burgundy leather Tom Ford shoes. He wasn't wearing any socks. The old guy had a little swag. I quickly diverted back to the subject at hand.

"Yeah, that's her. This place is some shit. They denied me my rights, no calls and no visits, the food is terrible," I said as my mind plotted. If I could get her in here, it was going down. She was a real ride or die chick and I needed her to rally all the support I could get to attend my hearing.

Makita was a hood chick with business sense and a college education. Her dad was the infamous Jack Penny, a legendary gangster. He had been murdered by rivalries, but before then he was a big kingpin when she was a teenager. As they say, the fruit doesn't fall too far from the tree and that was true in her case, which is why we broke up in the first place and I ended up with Sunday. Makita was too fast; I was too slow. Girls mature faster than dudes, she was running laps around me as a teenager. Plus, at a very young age she had a mentor, her legendary dad. My mentor was the streets and a teenage mom that raised me alone. I was a bastard; I never knew who my dad was.

I called her Knight because she was black as night, beautiful with long legs and a banging body with ass for days. She was a chick that thought very much like a man and acted like one, too. When we broke up, we were teenagers and, though she was young, she was running a crew of older chicks like a pro. They were doing all kind of crimes: fraudulent credit card schemes, identity theft and stealing out high-end stores, as well as robbing and setting dudes up to be murked. She was obsessed with getting money, just like her dad had been even though it sent him to an early grave. When I introduced her to my mom, the two got along, but it was nothing like when my mom first met Sunday. The two quickly formed a bond that was inseparable.

When I met Sunday, I was hustling and she was a schoolgirl: innocent, pristine with college ambitions. She was into her schoolbooks and Makita was into both while hitting more licks than me. They were actually close friends until the street life called Makita when her father was murdered. Until that moment, she was a straight A student and then she got caught up with a bunch of chicks that was doing all kinds of illegal shit. Once, while I was at her crib, chilling, some nigga pulled up and shot up her mom's crib behind some shit that she had started.

It became clear to me that Sunday was who I needed to be with. She was not just more laid back and beautiful with a big ass, but she was a chick that knew how to let a man be a man; as long as I didn't fuck shit up. She was a rider who had faith in me as long as I continued being a man worth holding down. After moving on with Sunday, I slowly built my empire, one ounce of coke at time, but I was safe with it, unlike Makita. She was making major money, but she was moving fast and reckless.

When I was driving around in a box Chevy, Makita was driving a candy-red AMG Benz convertible. Her crew was running the streets, pulling capers and making more money than they could spend. It was all good until they caught a body in an elaborate scheme. A sophisticated jewelry store heist went terribly wrong. The manager, a Jewish man in his late 50s with an appetite for young black girls, met one of Makita's girls, Dayja, at a Days Inn hotel for sex. The crew was waiting in a closet and as soon as he took his clothes off, he was ambushed and beaten with a hammer, and forced to give them all the security codes to the store and combinations to the safes.

They had got away with over nine million in jewelry and cash but when the body of the store manager was found floating in a lake, the data inside his cellphone lead authorities to Dayja, who had some of the jewelry stashed in her home. Eventually, the entire crew of girls were arrested, except for Makita, the mastermind. At the time, Makita was enrolled at Florida State University studying criminal law, so she had covered her ass properly with the perfect alibi.

"They haven't allowed you any visits outside of me?" my lawyer asked sternly with an arched brew.

"Nah, and no calls either. They got me in segregation. This is the 'hole'; no visits, no TV, no books to read. Nothing."

"Under the 8th Amendment of the U.S. constitution, you have the right to a phone call and a visit. I'm on it," he said sternly as he rose. After gathering his papers and depositing them back into his briefcase, he walked over and banged on the door, asking to speak to the sergeant on duty.

I was escorted back to my cell by two burly black ass officers, one of them had an attitude but the other was cool as shit. I noticed both of his ears were pierced and his arms were tatted, he looked barely in his twenties. His name tag read, 'Officer Jones'.

Not even an hour later, Officer Jones arrived in front of my cell wheeling a cart with a phone on the top. Since I was in segregation, I wasn't allowed to use the phone outside my cell like everyone else. Opening the tiny slot on my cell door, he pushed the receiver through and propped it open so I could dial on the keypad.

"Here you go, Mr. Shields. Just holla at me when you're finished. I get off work at five o'clock," he said with a hunt of a smile and began to walk away.

"Am I able to get visits now?" I asked sincerely.

"Definitely. I'ma make sure to check on that now. I just wanna tell you that I know who you are. My brotha and I got respect for you. I heard a lot 'bout you and the John Doe Boys," he beamed with a broad smile as he wiped at the sweat on his forehead.

I ignored his statement, I wasn't impressed. At the end of the day, he was a cop as far as I was concerned. I had a good vibe about him, but I still kept my mouth shut.

Moments later, I was able to check in on my moms, happy to hear that she was clean after the drug issue that she'd dealt with for years and all during my childhood. As much money as I'd made, she never asked me for shit other than a grandbaby so that she could have a second chance at being a mom.

Next, I called Makita. When she first answered, I heard a nigga in the background but that was none of my business. Even though she felt that I was obligated to be with her if I ever made it home, she was a free agent at the moment.

"I'm in Atlanta and I want you to come see me. I was granted an evidentiary appeal and I like my chances. If possible, bring me something. It's been a minute since I've been able to hear a friendly voice," I said, discreetly asking for her to bring me a burner phone.

"You lyin'! Where you at?" she screamed.

I could hear the patter of feet like she was running around the house. Then there was a deep baritone voice in the background that I briefly heard again but couldn't discern what was being said.

"I'm at the United States Penitentiary on 601 McDonough. The Feds holding me here until I go to court tomorrow. I'm comin' home like I told you. No cap," I bragged with a smile, waiting for her to respond.

Suddenly, the phone got silent.

"I'll be up there, but I also have to tell you something."

I frowned, hearing the grimness in her voice.

"What? Listen, I know you got a nigga and I ain't sweatin' that shit. Just let me tap that ass one time and I'm good." I was joking and I knew she was about to hit me back with some slick shit.

"Like hell! As long as I been waiting, you'll be doing more than just tapping this. I need a ring on my finger," she said, giddily.

I couldn't help but smile. Some things never changed. Makita stayed with the smart-ass comments.

"That's a tall order," I responded.

"Then fill it, nigga."

"We will see about all that."

"I'm on my way up there now with what you asked for. And then... we also have to talk about some other things."

The tone of her voice bothered me. I wanted to know what was so serious that she needed to speak to me in person. I hoped she wasn't serious about me making her wifey because that wasn't about to happen. I owed her and she had put in a bunch of work—more than I could have ever expected anyone to do, especially a chick. However, the fact still remained, no matter how much I tried to ignore it, my heart was still with Sunday.

***

An hour later, Officer Jones came to the cell and he was all excited.

"King, you got a visit and, boy, you really broke the mold with her," he gibed.

I knew he was talking about Makita's big butt, sexy black ass. He handcuffed me and escorted me out the cell. I did a replay as my mind continued to churn.

What was it she needed to talk to me about?

I was headed for visitation when I spotted the orderly, Keith, mopping the floor outside the officer's station. I dipped my head to greet him.

Throwing up the deuces, he smiled, "I got you."

I walked away, feeling light-hearted, relieved and hype about finally seeing a familiar face. However, nothing could have prepared me for what Makita had to tell me but once it was out, murder, rage, and destruction ravaged my brain. I was ready to kill a lot of people.

Chapter Six

K͂ing

I was escorted into a small booth, about the size of a closet. There was a big plexiglass window and a metal chair attached to the wall in front of the window. Adjacent to it was a phone that looked ancient, like it dated back to the 1940. The graveyard-gray walls were peeling paint. A sordid smell of cheap disinfectant and piss in the air heavy my nostrils.

Strangely, it was quiet. The first thing I did was look for security cameras. There wasn't any as far as I could see but that didn't mean they weren't there watching. I waited for Makita as I drummed my fingers on the metal desk in front of me, then hopped down and did a bunch of push ups.

The hell did she need to tell me? my mind wondered.

When Makita finally made her appearance, she blew my mind. She was dressed in a white tight Prada dress made out of some type of cotton material that clung to her figure. It was low-cut, her sensuous breasts were nearly exposed. I couldn't help but stare at her nipples the size of strawberries as they protruded forward, bouncing animated with her every step. Her hair was coiffured and long, with some type of reddish tint at the end as it elegantly cascaded over her left shoulder down to her supple breast.

Then she smiled with radiant splendor. It was faint but enough to display her perfect ivory teeth. She had high cheekbones and chatoyant eyes that could both captivate and mesmerize. What was must stunning about her was her walk. It was more like a gyrating strut, with a lot of oomph. She was provocative and sexy with a fat, round ass and hips that seduced men.

"Hi, Knight. Long time no see," I hinted at with humor.

This was still a business meeting, sort of anyway. I just needed to keep everything in prospective, even though she was a chick I used to smash many years ago and I knew she had expectations of us. I know that would never be happening, I just didn't' have the courage to tell her, even though anything could happen in the future.

"Good to see you, King," she said in a sultry voice as her eyes traveled over me chiseled chest and arms.

"The feeling is mutual."

"You still calling me 'Knight', I see." She smiled.

"So, tell me what's up. What were you talkin' 'bout on the phone?"

Her eyes darkened somberly as she lowered her head, as if forlorn. For some reason, she could no longer look at me.

That day, Makita nearly crushed me when she told me that Sunday was in the hospital, pregnant and fighting for her life, along with her fiancé, Caesar. The grim details threw me off but then she told me that the streets were saying that The John Doe Boys, under my command, were responsible for the attempted hit on them.

To make things worse, I also learned that several of our trap houses had been robbed and that Gunner, my childhood friend and a person I would lay my life on the line for, was possibly responsible for the robberies. My second in command, Shotti, was robbed for millions in product and money, and everyone inside the trap was killed but him. The shit seemed suspect to me, but I couldn't be sure.

But what was really killing me was what she'd told me about Sunday.

It felt like my soul melted.

"Damn," I muttered as my heart sank to the pit of my gut. I hunched down in my seat like the air had been let out of me.

"Whoever did it tried to make it look like a robbery. It may have been, but it was just too brutal. It made national news, even went viral. They been posting her pictures all over the media."

Silence.

I racked my brain for moment as the clamor of institutional noises enveloped us.

"What happened to the baby?" I finally asked as I massaged my temples. My head was suddenly throbbing with a headache.

"They may have to deliver it early. Sunday isn't responding to anything. Word is, if she were to live, she would more than likely be a vegetable."

"A vegetable... That's fucked up," I groaned.

As I mopped at my faced with weary hands, I felt my heart beating hard in my chest. This was too much to take in and I was unable to continue hiding it. Why should I? I had spent nearly eight years of my life with Sunday. The entire time I had been languishing in prison, I dreamed about her and envisioned her—us—in love, like we used to be even while confined in my concrete hell. My dreams about her and the moments we shared was the only thing that made my time bearable.

"I know you still love her," she pressed, trying to pick me for information.

I sighed and leaned forward. She was testing my patience. I wasn't concerned with any of this jealous chick shit that she was on after what I'd just learned that Sunday was going through. However, in that moment, I was in no position to piss her off. I needed Makita's help. So instead of going off on her, I expelled a deep sigh and placed my elbows on the metal table between us.

"So, do you?"

"Do I what?"

"Do you still love her? Because this 'ride or die' shit I'm doing, holding you down while you do a bid, ain't no charity shit. I'm tryna be that bitch you consider for putting a ring on her finger, babies out her womb, buy a big ass house in the suburbs in Buckhead, all that shit. I lost you before, I ain't trying to do it again," she said with so much passion I had to look at her twice.

"Prison taught me a lot. It taught me to always be there for the ones who have held me down and you're one of those people. I'll always appreciate that, and I'll always look out for you. But you can't be pushing me to put no rings on your finger when we both know you got a man at home waiting for you."

She bowed her head and cut her eyes away from mine. For a quick moment she was caught off-guard, but she recovered pretty fast.

"How you know I got a man? How you know I haven't been saving this pussy for you?"

"Fuck outta here," I chuckled and then gave her an even look. "Women who look like you don't go long without being piped down but I'm not holding that against you. A real nigga doing time can't ask a chick to be stronger than him, and if I was out on the bricks, I would be dicking hoes down." I shrugged because it was true. I was just being honest and that was one of the things Makita always liked about me.

"Just don't get pregnant and don't fuck none of my enemies, that's all I've ever asked you. But you can fuck a friend though, because that means they was disloyal and wasn't really a friend to begin with. For niggas like that, a bitch always gets them killed in the end."

She looked skeptical. "I don't understand that."

"Ok, that's on you. All I ask you is to just keep it one thousand with a nigga."

A nervous expression covered her face before she spoke again. "Right before you caught this case, you made a trip. We spoke about this before... I think I can flip that work that you got for you."

The offer was tempting because I knew she was good for it and could definitely flip it better than any nigga in the streets could. However, my gut was telling me that wasn't the move to make. Plus, I had a good chance that I would be released. If that happened, I could flip it on my own.

"Nah, I'm good over here. So just forget all about that. There is no need to mention it again."

"But there is a chance that you won't make..."

She stopped short of her statement, but I knew she was talking about the very real chance that I wouldn't make it back out. The chance I would die or be executed in prison.

I nodded and simply replied, "Real niggas take chances every day. Some of them you live with and some you die with."

Leaving that topic hanging, we continued with small talk until Officer Jones came to take me back to my cell. To be honest, I was more than happy to go. After hearing about Sunday, the only thing I wanted was to be alone with my thoughts.

****

Later that evening, Kevin slid an ounce of Loud under my cell door that he said Makita had stashed in the women's bathroom for me, along with the burner phone. I couldn't help but laugh because she knew me so well. I hadn't smoked weed in years and you would have to be a smoker to really realize just how appreciative I was to have some after hearing the news about Sunday. I had something to get my mind right, and I was thankful for that, because the next day was going to be a living hell. Nothing in the world could have prepared me for what happened next.

The Loud should have helped relieve the stress, but I couldn't seem to get Sunday off my mind no matter how hard I tried. And to think someone had started the rumor that the John Doe Boys and myself were behind the treacherous shit that happened to her and her fiancé. Yeah, I didn't like that nigga and I would have bitch slapped him if he ever ran up on me, but I wished no man ill will over a chick. I couldn't help but wonder, was I being set up by the same people who murdered Tony Span, his wife and my goddaughter?

After stopping up the vent in the ceiling that blew out air as well as the crack under my door to mute the smell of Loud, I lit the blunt and took a long puff. My mind was all over the place. I needed to get out. I needed to see Sunday. I needed for this to all be over with.

I quickly tried to push Sunday out my mind and focus on what I would face the next day, but it was hard—really hard. The evidentiary hearing was going to be my last chance at freedom. It was the first step to getting my life back, redeeming myself and possibly starting over; maybe even with Sunday if she could somehow make it out the hospital. I knew it was a long shot but again, I had a chance. There was hope and that was all I had.

****

The next day after I had showered, I stashed the leftover weed and burner inside my mattress and waited for what felt like eternity, until it was time to leave. Finally, the guards came to get me. They showed up twelve-deep, led by a redneck lieutenant with a heavily starched white shirt and a gold badge as he barked orders.

Hours later, I was dressed in a carrot-orange jail jumpsuit, seated in front of the judge with my lawyer right next to me. To my shock, the courtroom was packed. Nearly every seat was filled with a member of the John Doe Boy gang. They were deep, wearing their royal blue colors, and so was the security; the cops were wall-to-wall like they were expecting something to jump off. There was also a handful of media. I recognized some and a few even spoke to me. In their eyes, I was the infamous hood gangsta, known as King Banks.

I saw Makita dressed to impress, seated right behind me at the defense table. My mom and other family were there, including my little sister, Nikki. We had not spoken in nearly a year after her boyfriend had fabricated lies against me to get a time cut, but since then we had made up. At the end of the day, she was my sister and I loved her.

As I turned my head to wave at my moms, I spotted Gunner, my lieutenant. He looked disheveled, his cheeks were sunken, his eyes were gaunt. He had lost a considerable amount of weight, like maybe he was sick or something, but he showed love, shouted my name and repped our set. I nodded my head in greeting to him but, in the back of my mind, I couldn't help but think about what had been said about him robbing me.

"JDBs!" he shouted aloud.

As soon as he said it, the entire courtroom erupted with the sing-song chants of 'JDBs' in the courtroom. The bailiffs and cops moved around, telling them to cut it out and my attorney gave me a stern expression, letting me know what he was thinking. This wasn't a good look for me right now. I quickly found Bulletproof and Dolo in the back of the courtroom. They were the incorrigible ring leaders, hyping everyone up, until I caught their attention with a piercing glare and mouthed, "Chill! Stop the bullshit." They obeyed.

What stood out to me was when I turned and saw Shotti on the other side of the courtroom. He could barely meet my gaze, but he did throw up our gang sign, an image of a gun: raising two fingers and a thumb, with both hands. However, the fact that he could hardly look at me was an instant concern.

On my right, seated at the prosecutors table, was Donald Lee, the Fed's lead prosecutor. He was a huge white man of stature, standing about six-foot-six and over three hundred pounds with broad shoulders. He looked like he may have been a linebacker in his younger days. He wore thin glasses that looked too small for his big Elmer Fudd-shaped head.

Donald Lee was known for logistic brilliance in law tactics and unscrupulous borderline illegal behavior, both in the courtroom and out. They did a feature on him on A & E some years back about how he'd held back evidence that would have freed several innocent black men in six cases. It was a wonder that he was still able to practice law.

Federal Judge Regina Duncan was elegant, regal black woman with mahogany skin and a beautiful face. Her black hair had fringes of gray, tied to the back in a bun. She was a buxom woman that looked to be anywhere between thirty-four to forty-four, providing evidence to the saying that 'black don't crack'. She practiced law with a no-nonsense approach as she banged her gavel.

"Quiet in the courtroom or I will have each of you escorted out of here!"

There was a ripple of voices as the courtroom noise suddenly came to a lull.

"Prosecuting attorney Mr. Lee, I see here in your evidentiary records that there has been an addendum added to it," the judge said as she looked at some papers in front of her desk.

Lee stood and adjusted his pants to conceal his potbelly.

"Yes, I needed to add for the court records that the little four-year-old girl had possibly been sexually assaulted."

Disgruntled voices erupted throughout the courtroom as the judge frowned and looked over at me. My lawyer was on his feet with the quickness.

"Your Honor, the prosecution is just now making this known but, also, these are inflammatory statements. They have no relevance in this courtroom proceeding but only to damage my client. Also, this evidence, even if it was relevant, should have been placed into the discovery for me to review."

"I disagree, Your Honor. This is relevant because under title code eighteen, I can make the court known of anything that may be criminal and circumstantial to the hearing."

"That is not how the law is supposed to be applied. If the court will allow me time, I can prove so with legal statures that say otherwise!" my attorney argued back. The two attorneys exchanged more heated words before the judge finally banged her gavel.

"Enough! Or I will have you two in contempt of court in my courtroom."

There was a volley of words exchanged, legal terms and lingo that I knew nothing about, but what I did understand was that my lawyer was fully engaging the prosecutor. Judging from the argument, he appeared to be winning. The judge continued to agree in his favor and the more it happened, the more hope I gained. I stole an opportunity to glance over at my mom.

"You are coming home," she mouthed. I read her lips and smiled.

Nobody knew my old girl held the key to everything. She had been the real glue that not only held me together, but my entire empire. I had purchased her a home in Roswell, Georgia, in a bogus name, under a company cooperation just as the rich white folks do. No one but me, her and a lawyer knew about that it.

Again, I looked over at Shotti and he continued to stare straight ahead, as if he was distant. However, it was his expression that told me everything I needed to know. Gangsters like myself had to function off gut instincts and street savviness or our lifespan would be cut short by a timely demise. Right then, my instincts were telling me that my once good friend could have betrayed me in some way. I wasn't a cardinal saint; I had committed crimes before, but only in retaliation or self-defense; never had I harmed an entire family or a child.

I made a mental note to send word out immediately to have him watched. I wasn't sure who had set me up yet and everyone was going to be a suspect until I started my process of elimination. I had learned that when bodies started dropping, people started talking.

Suddenly, the judge looked up and stared directly at me then asked the bailiff for a fifteen-minute recess before returning with her decision. That was the first time she looked at me and I saw kindness in her eyes as I watched her rise from her desk and gather some papers to leave.

As soon as she left, I turned to speak with my mother and some of my crew. Bulletproof and Dolo both tried to walk over to me, but instantly, the bailiff rushed them along with several police who had been added to the court proceeding for extra security. There was some minor pushing and shoving. They both moved back to their seats but not before Bulletproof, the most aggressive of the crew, announced "JDBs! We four thousand deep in Atlanta alone." He was rewarded with hoots and chants.

I flinched, telling them to chill. At the time, what I didn't realize was outside the federal courtroom, in the streets was a spectacle like never seen before. There were thousands of supporters and people from our hood and even other states that sympathized with our organization. The John Doe Boys had turned into a movement, and it was mostly due to social media networking and organizing

We must have drove the bailiffs crazy inside the courtroom, there was loud talking and yelling, people calling my name. Somebody threw a balled-up piece of paper at the prosecutor, hitting him in the back of his head. He jumped to his feet, yelling and arrogantly asked, who did it?

All I could do was look on in dismay. This was not helping my cause, but I had to admit their presence was needed and the streets were watching along with some of the rest of the world.

Moments later the judge walked back in, her stoic demeanor attentive and alert. There was a sudden stifling silence as a murmur of voices lulled to a quiet. The tension in the room was tight as a rope.

The judge took her seat and glowered at the courtroom like she knew about the loud ruckus in her absence. She then went into her legal introduction as it related to her opinion of the case that would ultimately change my life forever, the courtroom had drawn so quiet you could hear a pin drop.

In the background behind me I heard somebody praying and look behind me, it was my mama, she was reading her Bible.

I held my breath.

"This case troubles me and I must admit I have my concerns, which caused me to do extensive research in studying case law. One of the things that disturbs me was that recently an estimated three thousand cases were slated for re-examination that were like this very case which dealt with FBI hair and fiber analysis this is being used more and more since DNA testing became widely available. So far, almost two thousand cases have been reviewed and were found to have flaws, over ninety percent. In some cases, the misuse of evidence was used to convict innocent people."

The judge then glowered at Lee. Instantly, I felt a sense of relief as I heard my mama in the background say, "Yes, Lord, bring him home!"

I cut my eyes over at Shotti and for the first time I saw concerned etched on to his face. I suddenly had doubts about his guilt.

"However, in this particular case right here the other evidence speaks loudly. Given the circumstances, the defendant didn't have an alibi, and did have ties with the slain family, and that his girlfriend at the time just happened to walk in and discover the bodies. I found this to be more than circumstantial, and not just that, the little girl in question who may or may not have been sexually molested, the court has no choice but to take that into account, as well as the defendant's background and prior criminal history. It is alleged that the defendant is the leader and organizer in the RICO crime act. To date, there have been three police officers brutally murdered and a host of civilians."

"Your honor, that has nothing to do with my client," my lawyer interrupted.

The judge stopped talking and glared at him. There was a pregnant pause, then she continued.

"For these reasons, I owe a duty to my courtroom and my country to uphold the jurisprudence of the law as I see fit. With that being said, I have no choice but to rule in favor of the prosecution, because I don't see sufficient evidence to rule in favor of the defendant," the judge said looking directly at me and banged her gavel.

Instantly, there was upheaval. Someone threw a small trash can across the courtroom. Several bailiffs rushed over, and there was shouting and shoving. When a cop ran over, pulled out a stun gun, and shot one of the crew, things quickly escalated. The cops and the bailiff were outnumbered, and soon there was a huge melee with punches being thrown. All I could do was sit there stunned, in sheer disbelief. Then I turned to check on my mom and sister. They were still there, but I noticed that Shotti was gone. Then, I felt bodies topple over on into the desk, one of my crew was wrestling with the officer trying to take his gun.

"Fuck!"

I was supposed to be leaving prison. I was supposed to be free, or at least have good grounds for an appeal. Even though I had done a lot of fucked up shit in my day, I didn't deserve this. I looked around the courtroom at the melee which had erupted into pure pandemonium as the bailiffs rushed over assaulting people. Even the media that had shown up was involved; several of them had got caught up in the fight.

Members of my crew, Thug, Spank and Kilo, were on their feet getting it in, like a street brawl as they fought with the police toe-to-toe, throwing blows. Gunner had his back against the wall, and Makita was only a few feet away standing with my sister and mom. The terror of it all was etched on their faces. I felt several people grab me roughly and I was yanked up out my chair. The bailiffs were rough handling me as if I was the culprit as they called for backup on their radio.

"I'll file for an appeal. She can't do this; the United States Court of Appeals is going to toss this case," my lawyer yelled as he ducked from something being thrown.

Though his words were hopeful, I knew better. I could see it in his eyes; they were dead like I would be once they executed me. The United States Courts of Appeal rarely accepted cases like mine and, when they did, only 1% of defendants prevailed after waiting years to be heard.

My emotions were numb as I was damn near dragged across the courtroom by the bailiffs. I stole a glance at my mom as she cried in her hands, releasing maudlin tears that hurt my soul. Not too far away was Makita and my sister. Makita was emotionless but her eyes were red, like how people look when they're devastated, shocked beyond their mind, and don't know what to say. For over three years she had been visiting me, running my business and holding me down. She, too couldn't even meet my gaze. This would be end of the road for us, for me, and the life we hoped to renew together.

As I reached the door to the inmate holding facility adjacent to the courtroom, right next to the judge's chamber. Behind me, I could hear my mom call my name, in the midst of uttering a litany of prayers. She cried right along with my sister. They were drenched in a river of tears. Several other people called out my name, chanting together in unison. That was when everything went bizarre, like I was in a trance, moving in surrealistic motion as the bailiffs rushed me to the holding cell. The ruckus of noise in the courtroom continued.

The Federal marshals were already inside waiting. They chatted idly as I was escorted in. It appeared they were absolutely oblivious to the fisticuff that was going on in the very next room and after a few seconds, I could see why. Either the courtroom was soundproof, or the room was; you couldn't hear a thing from inside. My eyes scanned the room as I was told to sit and did so with difficulty. My hands were still cuffed in front of me.

"We are having a problem in the courtroom. A riot..." The bailiff cut his eyes at me as he filled in the marshals. "It began after his appeal was denied. Can one of you come assist? The crowd is pretty large."

"I got it," one of the marshals replied. "You stay with him."

Together, the bailiff and marshal both rushed out with their hands on their weapons. I got a glance outside the door; it was almost empty outside. From the look of it, as soon as they had dragged me down the hall, the crew must have taken off for the exits. It was a smart move because the police had surely called for backup.

Two marshals remained in the room with me, but they weren't at all concerned with the courtroom proceedings, much less me. My mind was still in a frenzy, I had been so close to coming home but, now, so far. Either way, I knew that I just couldn't let them take me back to that cage.

"Since I'm in here, can I get these off?" I asked, lifting my cuffed hands in the air.

The marshals turned to me, as if they were just seeing me for the first time since I'd entered the room, and then one nodded.

"Yeah, okay."

He took out his keys to remove my handcuffs as he continued to converse with his buddy about a vacation that he and his family were taking next week to the Grand Canyon. Their light-hearted conversation was a direct contrast to my inner thoughts.

I'm going to die in prison...

They were about to take me back to the dreadful, draconian penitentiary and my life would be doomed. Over.

"Do you want some coffee to take on the road?" I heard one of the marshals ask the other.

"Yes," the other one replied. I was too deep in my thoughts to know which was which.

With my head down, I heard steps as someone walked away, pausing only a moment to unlock a heavy steel door before continuing on.

I was left alone with the other marshal, who was scrolling through something on his phone. My record and reputation while locked up was probably what had them so off-guard. I'd never been a problem, not even once, unless provoked. His casual behavior toward me would work in my favor. The cuffs were off, and I rubbed my raw wrist while searching around the room.

Suddenly, a desperate thought emerged in the dark crevice of my mind as a plan began to unravel. It was a desperate one, but desperate times called for desperate measures. What I was thinking was nothing short of suicide, but it was my last chance at freedom. The marshal had an athletic build and muscular frame like a wrestler. He was a few inches taller than me and a few pounds heavier. From just the look at him, I knew it wouldn't be easy.

Just as he moved to place his phone back into his pocket, I hit him with a quick right hook with all my might, square on his chin. He staggered and almost fell but recovered fast and then dropped his head to run into me like a ram. The force damn near knocked me off my feet. I was propelled backwards. I was not prepared for this. When his arms began to windmill throwing punches, I was violently slammed against a wall, causing some pictures to tumble as our fight ensued.

There was a loud crash as we knocked over a table with a computer stationed on top. I managed to get off a few good punches, but it didn't see to fade him. In fact, when he rose, his nose was bloody and his face was crimson red with blood, but it was like pure adrenaline was rushing through him as he continued to swing wildly.

I may have bitten off more than I could chew.

The white boy knew how to fight. He swung again and we locked like crabs in a bucket—a fight to the death. His confidence got the better of him when he dropped his guard just to get in a good punch and nearly lost his balance. Taking the opportunity, I leaped and managed to get my arms around his neck in a partial headlock and squeezed, cutting off the air to his windpipe. He started resisting, punched me in my back and tried a desperate swing for my face, then attempted to gouge my eyes out with fingers stiff like talons.

I choked him harder…

He continued to resist. Until, finally, his strength was starting to wane, and his body began to tremble. I could hear him struggle to breathe so I squeezed harder.

I heard him gag, then begin to choke as his arms flailed like a fish out of water.

I choked him even harder.

That's when I felt something crack. It was his neck. His body went limp and I heard a gasp escape his lungs—his last breath. I let him go and he fell to the floor with his neck broken. I looked around for a way to exit out the building. My heart was beating so hard. There was a back exit that I remembered coming through with tunnels and other passageways, but I would have to get out of there fast before the other marshal returned.

Just as I looked around for a weapon, as if on cue, the courtroom door opened.

I was busted!

It was his partner and he was holding two cups of coffee in his hands, struggling to balance them while using one foot to tug open the heavy door. Thankfully, he hadn't yet seen our scuffle or his dead partner's body lying on the other side of the door with his neck broken.

I knew that I had to think fast. On top of the desk in front of me was a fax machine or some type of heavy similar apparatus. I reached out and snatched it up as fast as I could before lunging it at him. The machine narrowly missed as he looked up in time and ducked just in time, causing it to crash against the wall. He dropped both cups and dived at me just as I sprung forward at him. We clashed like two Titanics, only he was taller and outweighed me by nearly fifty pounds.

I was slammed backward, rammed into a cabinet and, instantly, the wind was knocked out of me. After already enduring the fight with his partner, I was nearly no match for him. He hit me with a vicious hard right that sent me reeling with more stars and stripes exploding in my brain, like a kaleidoscope of color.

"You motherfucker! I'ma fucking kill you!" He sneered with feral lips pressed tight across his face as he reached back to punch me again. As I struggled, trying to get him off of me, I could tell by the expression on his face that his intent was deadly. He wanted to kill me.

He swung.

Wham!

It would have been a punishing blow, had I not managed to move, but the blow still grazed my face with enough force to cause new pain to ricochet through my body. As I moved with my back flat on the desk and objects falling to the floor, I couldn't believe that no one had walked through the door.

My strength was waning, and I didn't see any way out of my current predicament. As it was, I'd already killed his partner, giving him a license to murder me in self-defense.

"You black motherfucker. I'm going to kill you!" the marshal raged, lifting his fist once more.

Just then, as I was planning a counter move, I saw something on the end of the desk only a few inches away. It was a pair of scissors.

The officer swung and I moved out of the way, closer to the metal object. When he reached back to swing again, so did I. With my weapon in hand, I plunged the scissors in his left eye causing blood to splatter like I had just slammed a sledgehammer onto a tomato. He howled like a wounded animal as his one good eye filled with terror. He tried to speak, he was in utter shock, but no words came out of his mouth. He staggered around as if someone had just turned the lights out before finally toppling over and falling to the floor, next to his comrade. His body trembled as life left his body. Though he wasn't gone yet, he didn't have much time left.

Neither did I. I had killed two federal marshals, so if I didn't escape now, there was no way I would make it out of this courtroom alive. Once my new crimes were discovered, I'd be killed on the spot.

After taking the officer's weapons, I rushed over and took the clothes off of the first officer's body and pulled them on. My face was still drenched in blood and as I stood and listened intently for any and every sound, expecting at any minute for a storm trooper of arm forces to rush in.

As I stepped over the two bodies, prepared to open the door and make my excursion into the unknown, I hesitated momentarily and closed my eyes, shutting them tight. With both weapons in my hands, I muttered my hood anthem which was also considered the gospel to a gangster.

"I'd rather be carried by six then judged by twelve."

Hearing a sound, I looked down at the handle when I realized where it as coming from. Someone was about to walk in.

With my fingers pressed against the trigger of each Glock in my hand, I took a few steps back, bit down on my bottom lip and prepared to face my worst nightmare.

Chapter Seven

~
Sunday

"You have no idea how much I love you..."

Lifting my head, I looked up, frowning slightly when I saw the way the intensity in King's stare. Feeling nervous suddenly, I shifted, sitting up on the bed as I stared into his eyes. With one hand, I smoothed down my top over my belly, nearly flat with only a small bulge from the baby growing inside.

I was only three months pregnant and, though this child wasn't expected, it was wanted and had already been smothered in love. As soon as King heard the news of me being pregnant, he went out and bought over a thousand dollars' worth of clothes for his unborn child. All clothes meant for a boy because he was certain that I was giving birth to our son. I told him that it was bad luck to buy anything before I made it over three months, but he didn't care. He was excited and, as much as I tried to play it cool, so was I.

A love like this was meet for the heavens, created by God almighty, I couldn't have been happier and so was King. For the first time, he was actually open to considering if the child was a girl and the possibilities of what we would name her. One day he slipped and said he wanted to buy a big five-bedroom home in a plush neighborhood in Alpharetta and get married before I had the baby. I was elated, even though he had been drinking, smoking and we had just had sex and were pillow talking. King was a man that didn't just speak words into existence, he made things happen in a major way. The next day when I breeched the subject of us getting married, he tactfully tried to skirt around it by saying he was just playing but I know he wasn't. The cat was officially out of the bag.

August 7th is a day I would never forget. I had to beg, plead and threaten King to go with me to the doctor for an ultrasound. It had been like pulling teeth, but he finally agreed. That day, we drove with the top down in his sky-blue Bentley Coupe. The wind was in our hair, the air was filled with merriment and intoxicating intimacy. For some reason, King couldn't keep his hands off me.

In so many ways, he showed that he was excited about being a father even though he would never admit it. Normally, he would spend every night hustling hard in the streets with his crew but, lately, he had been really engrossed with the idea of having a child and possibly settling down. Many nights that he would be out, he spent with me instead. He would even watch 'soft ass chick lit movies' with me, as he referred to them. I was learning that even though he was a thug and had been accused of some despicable things, people could change. Love makes people change and he was showing that to me.

We arrived at Dr. Jenkins' office as scheduled and, as usual, I pretended not to notice the female staff members craning their necks to get a look at King. A few even spoke to him and ignored me, like I wasn't the pregnant one who came in for a checkup.

Dr. Jenkins was a middle-aged woman with a cinnamon-complexion, pleasant smile and a great professional demeanor. She also spoke with a distinct dialect like she could possibly be from one of the islands. That day, we shared jubilant conversation; it was one of the happiest days of our life. Although I couldn't wait to see our baby, my stomach was growling. I was so ready to trick King into taking me to the Cheesecake Factory to eat afterwards.

As the doctor applied some type of gel to my belly, I lay on the table staring into the dimness of the screen as King sat next to me like a proud father to be. His smile was beautiful, radiant and strong as he too looked at the gray mask of matter on the screen, an anatomy of a fetus. A human life that we'd created through love. The chatter of our voices as we brought up our ideas of would-be baby names was the current theme of our conversation, along with the cackle of suppressed laughter.

Until...

That little wand that was supposed to make magic had seemed to be failing us as it strolled across the surface of my brown, lubricated, belly in search of a tiny heartbeat. Our laughter died and was replaced by our stricken faces. We paused, anxious, as the doctor turned and stole a glance at the both of us, her expression stoic.

"Is everything alright?" I heard myself ask, but I wasn't immediately given an answer.

The wand continued to search.

I stopped breathing and feared the worst as I suddenly became conscious of something. There was an absence of a sound that I expected, and it instantly told me what was wrong. She couldn't find the baby's heartbeat!

Finally, King asked with his voice brazen, "Yo, what's going on doc?"

"I can't find a heartbeat," she said with dismay as her eyes looked between the both of us. Her movement across my stomach slowed as she lost hope.

"Keep looking for it! What you mean you can't find it?" King raised his voice, urging her on.

"King!" I admonished. I watched in horror as her hand moved across my stomach in search of something that should have been there. Life.

Finally, she stopped, and then turned and looked at us.

"I'm sorry. There is no heartbeat," she said with the straight face of a professional.

In my peripheral, I saw King's shoulders hunch as his hand mopped at his face filled with sudden despair and disbelief. The entire time I stared straight ahead, devastated with the fear of the inevitable looking me in the face as I looked at the screen in front of me.

I walked out of the doctor's office in a mental fugue as King held my hand. I could tell he took it harder than me, especially when the doctor was explaining how to get the remains of our child out of my womb.

"This is some fuckin' bullshit!" he'd exclaimed before kicking over a chair.

Surprisingly, Dr Jenkins remained calm and recommended that we might consider counselling. All I could do was nod my head. I was in a trance. It was hard for me to digest something my mind and heart weren't prepared for: the death of our unborn child.

That week, King bought me a top of the line E Class 350 Mercedes Benz and made it his business to shower me with gifts and affection. He even chartered a private jet to Paris. He was doing everything in his power to ease my mind from the tragedy of losing the child. In the meantime, he was coping in his own way.

The John Doe Boys was escalating rapidly. One night, I accidently walked in on him in the basement and his clothes were covered in blood. I pretended not to see it, but I did. My love for him was so strong that it blinded me. I had been with him since the age of fifteen, when he didn't have nothing but dope boy dreams, a gangsta's mentality and hood ambitions.

As promised, King got me pregnant again and three months in, I lost that baby, too. Once again, King blamed himself. It tormented him and he took it out on the streets. The violence started again, this time it was worse. Two of his rivals were found decapitated with their hands cut off and eyeballs gouged. It was horrific but it was also a retaliation move.

I never asked him about what I was hearing about him, but the streets were talking. Unconsciously, I was being groomed to be a gangsta's wife and one day a widow. You never knew what you would do for love, until tragedy hit. Then you find yourself doing things you couldn't even fathom doing before. Malik 'King' Shields broke my heart, but even to this day, I still loved him. Even as I lay in a hospital bed nearly dead and in a coma, I dreamed about him. I dreamed about what we had...

What we lost.

Monochromic lights and psychedelic montage flashbacks of King assaulted my brain as I lay in a state of catalepsy. My entire world strobed like I was floating in outer space. I could hear sounds: sycophant beeps droned, people talking. Someone was crying poignantly. Their voice was hysterical; I realized it was my mama.

"Sunday, baby, I know you can hear. Please, move your hand... your eyelids... something! Please Lord, help her!"

I tried to do as she asked but I couldn't. It felt like my entire body was paralyzed. Including my brain.

Then something terrifying dawned on me. My baby! What happened to my child? I tried to will myself to move again, but I couldn't. Then another daunting thought occurred to me. Where was Caesar? In all the haze, I couldn't remember much that happened before I got here.

I was helpless.

"I'm going to need for you to sign some papers, waivers, and a consent form to have her taken off the life support system if her condition continues to deteriorate once we remove the baby," the doctor said.

My mother must have just stared at him dumbfounded, because she didn't respond. Then I heard someone else in the room, muttering something under their breath.

"To be truthful," the doctor continued. "Things are looking grim. We think she has less than a two percent chance of making it and we are unsure of how the trauma of the shooting is going to impact the unborn child. However, we are about to attempt to perform an emergency cesarean to take the baby out. You really should consider taking her off life support."

"Dr... What did you say your name was again?" my mama asked in a stern, no-nonsense tone.

"I know he didn't say what I think he just said?" I heard another voice in the room say. I could vaguely recognize it.

"Dr. Stevens," the doctor responded curtly.

"Okay. Listen, Dr. Stevens, only God, my Lord in Heaven, can make a decision like that. As far as I'm concerned, if she is breathing then she is living. She is still alive, and she is coming home with me. So enough of that shit you're talking. Do you understand me?"

I couldn't believe I heard my Mama curse. She never cursed. I thought that maybe I was dead, or at least really close, as I eavesdropped on a conversation that I probably shouldn't have been hearing.

"As you wish, but this can be costly. There is the matter of bed space for the facility—"

"Are you serious? I don't give a damn about none of that. In fact, where are your superiors? I can't believe you just said that to me!" my mama snapped.

"Right, I know you just didn't say what I think you said! The fuck you mean, taking up bed space? This ain't no fuckin' prison, this is supposed to be a hospital!" the familiar voice said.

That's when it occurred to me who it was. My girl, Kelly. She was the other one I heard in the room sobbing. The last time I saw her was the day that I was shot right after he told me that I was fired for giving her free weed.

Suddenly, I heard a scuffle with a chair overturning.

"If you don't get your hands off me, I'm calling the police and having you arrested for assault!" the doctor protested.

"Lord, girl, let him go," my mama said. All I could hear around her was pushing and shoving.

"I should punch yo' white ass in the face!" Kelly vented some more.

I tried to move, open my eyes, move a leg, an arm, or even yell but nothing was moving. Then I heard footfall and a door slam shut.

"Child, why did you grab that man like that and shove him around? He almost tripped over the chair and hit his head on that machine." She was flustered.

"I don't care! My friend is dying and she's lying right there pregnant with a baby, that is possibly dying, too. Then on top of that, this man worried about some fuckin' bed space," Kelly retorted.

I could hear tears in her voice. She was pacing the room as she spoke.

"Listen," my mama began poignantly. "Violence ain't going to cure nothing. Violence is what got my babies here, her boyfriend in the room down the hall, and his brother murdered. This girl, my child, has been in a coma for nearly three weeks fighting for her life. If you want to fight, then help her fight!"

It hurt me to my core as, instantly, I had flashbacks of the killings. I remembered masked gunmen storming into my apartment, the name Daze, and a face with no mask...

"No, but this hurts me to my soul," Kelly said, still crying and sobbing.

"I know, but all we can do is leave it in the Lord's hands. We have to pray for her, Caesar, and the baby."

My mama's hand rested on my stomach, and it felt like that gave me life. Her touch caused my very soul to awaken. Only something as strong as a mother's endearing love for her child could do that. At first, there were a lot of white lights beckoning me, calling me to walk down what looked like a tunnel. But then I felt my soul being moved in the opposite direction and things started to get clearer. Like smoke evaporating and crystalizing, it felt like I had returned from someplace that I wasn't meant to come back from. Even though I couldn't move, it was emotional for me having my mother's hand on my belly, on my unborn child.

"Look! Look!" I heard Kelly exclaim, along with the sound of feet moving like she was jumping up and down.

"What is wrong with you? These people gon' kick you out if you don't stop it. I already know you high because I smell weed all over you," my mama said with aggravation.

"No, she is crying! Look on the side of her face, there are tears. Sunday is crying," Kelly shouted.

"Jesus help me, Lawd! She is!"

My mama grabbed my face and held it in her hands as she continued to cry.

"If you can hear me, baby, wake up. Please, wake up so I can take you and the baby home."

I tried to move, but I couldn't, my body wouldn't let me. I could hear and even smell my mama's sweet Jasmine perfume.

Just then the door opened. The sound of radios and the murmur of hospital sounds, along with the churr of walkie-talkies followed.

"There she is right there. I want her escorted off the premises immediately!"

Dr. Stevens had returned and must have brought with him police officers or something.

"You play-play ass officers better not put y'all fuckin' hands on me!" Kelly protested loudly.

"I am not a play police officer; I am hospital security. I'm sorry, ma'am, but you're going to have to leave the premises," the male voice said.

"Don't be sorry because I ain't going nowhere."

"Just stop it!" my mama protested, then added emotionally. "Doctor, come here. Look, she is crying."

Dr. Stevens walked over; I could feel his presence towering over me, palpable like a second layer of skin.

"She is," the doctor said softy. I felt a hand on my cheek. Then he began messing with the tubes in my arms, the EKG machine and, eventually, the breathing tube.

"Interesting. I am looking at her CT brain scans and, suddenly, there is activity," the doctor marveled.

"What is that?" my mother asked.

"It shows all the neurological injuries she suffered due to the trauma to her head. It's looking better, even though we were unable to remove the bullet. It was too close to her prefrontal cortex. That is where her ability to index memories would be and damage to that area would cause a list of other problems that are too long to name. There is the possibility that she will be blind in one eye, but the severe facial and skull damage could be surgically repaired, though costly."

"Yes, lawd!"

Blind in one eye... facial and skull damage, I repeated in the dark crevice of my mind.

"Ma'am, can you please come with me?" the security guard asked again.

"Man, if you don't get yo' short, midget ass on!" Kelly huffed with a dismissive wave of her hand.

"Let her stay," the doctor said, catching everyone off guard. "Something triggered a positive psychoneurosis in the patient, and it could have been the girl or her mom. They have both been by her bedside every day since she has been in the hospital," the doctor said.

"I know damn well you ain't just call me a girl. I'ma grown ass woman as you can see," Kelly snapped.

"I'm going to need to run some more tests. I also want some of my colleagues to help me, rarely has this happened before, but it's not uncommon for people to survive gunshot wounds to the head."

"It's called prayer and God," my mama said with ebullience.

"Well, we are going to need all of that tomorrow. Because of the trauma suffered to both mother and child, we are removing the baby early. We will do everything in our power to have a safe delivery and I will also let the father know about the procedure. He is still in intensive care; he, too, is very lucky to be alive. We are running tests on him. However, he still has all his cognitive abilities. We know he suffered some permanent damage and there is still the likely possibility of paralysis. He is definitely going to need a colostomy bag."

"Paralysis? Colostomy bag?" I heard my mama repeat.

"So, basically, Caesar going be wearing a shit bag," Kelly chimed in, as if to explain.

"Child, don't say it like that. I know what it is!"

I heard the doctor make some sort of grunt, then there were footsteps before a door opened, then closed.

Everything else became a cloud in my mind as I drifted back toward a light at the end of a long, dark tunnel. There really was something mystic in the light and it greeted me head-on like two ships in the night.

Chapter Eight

~ King

Four burly bailiffs walked in. One of them was mammoth with a big protruding gut that hung over his waist. He was the first to enter. His eyes stretched wide as he looked around the room at death and destruction. The other three bailiffs were not paying much attention, their chatter was about the prior courtroom upheaval.

"What the hell!" the first bailiff exclaimed, getting the rest of their attention as they all suddenly stopped. All eyes were on me. The first bailiff reached for his gun, but I moved faster with a shot to his leg.

Blocka!

The big .40 caliber weapon roared like a cannon. The bailiff shouted like a bitch and keeled over, landing to the floor with a thud.

The others immediately jumped to attention, reaching for their weapons. I had the ups on them, and it was apparent that my modus operandi was to shoot first, ask no questions. Judging from the bodies scattered on the floor and all the gory blood, they could clearly see I wasn't playing any games.

"Move over here. Put you fuckin' hands where I can see 'em or I'm going to blow your fucking brains out!" I gestured, waving the gun in their faces as I rushed over to relieve them of their weapons. The entire time, the bailiff was on the floor was moaning and groaning in agony.

I handcuffed them to a steel rod in the room that was connected to the concrete wall, the same kind of device that was designed to detain inmates at court who were wearing restraints. Instantly, they began to complain and started an uproar, complaining about the cramped space they were handcuffed inside.

"Either you deal with this or I can shoot each one of you in the dome," I reasoned, waving the gun.

I didn't want any more bloodshed, but I had to get out of there and fast. Though courtrooms were soundproof for privacy and public outbursts, I wasn't certain if that included the piercing sound of gunshots.

I would soon find out.

I was about to exit the room, and something suddenly occurred to me, I had almost made a huge blunder. Doubling back, I searched the bailiff's pockets and, sure as shit, they had their cell phones. I took them and made one last threat to come back and kill them all if they made any noise or tried to call for help. They wouldn't comply for long, but it would buy me a decent amount of time.

Moving stealthily, I slipped through the door that led to the courtroom with my eyes scanning my surroundings. My grim reality was daunting, but there was no turning back. Still, I was on edge, and my heart and mind were racing. I had no idea what to expect. The last time I was in the courtroom, it was filled with hundreds of people, most of them security and staff. There was only a matter of time before someone would discover the dead bodies and the handcuffed bailiffs.

After scanning the scene, I realized that I had no choice but to walk through another door adjacent to the courtroom because the back corridor that I traveled through with the marshals were fortified with armed police, sheriffs and FBI from other agencies that were transporting inmates back and forth to court. At the moment, many of them were attentively watching their prisoners, trying to keep them under control in light of all the ruckus that my supporters were commanding outside. The door next to the courtroom was my only option, but I'd have to walk out in the open to get to it. It was a bold move, but at that point I had nothing to lose and everything to gain.

Walking with intention, I stepped out from the holding facility and into the hall with both pistols stashed at my side, fully prepared to go out in a hail of gunfire. Luckily, no one seemed to pay much attention to me as I made my way to the door. Exhaling out a sharp breath, I quickly pulled on the handle to open it quickly before sliding inside.

There was someone in the room!

Just when I was about to start blasting on sight, I recognized who the person was. It was the stenographer and she had her back to me. She was an attractive, heavy-set woman who appeared to be in her forties. From the looks of it, she was oblivious to anything being out of place as she moved quickly, preparing to leave while placing large folders into large yellow envelopes. I quickly turned and pressed against the door that I walked in from as she made her way out of another across from where I stood. That was when I heard the sound of high heels approaching the door behind me.

Quickly, with a gun in each hand, prepared to go out kamikaze-style, I followed out the same exit the stenographer used and found myself inside another room.

What the fuck? The entire place was a maze.

To my side, there was a metal trash can and I deposited the cell phones that I'd taken from the bailiffs inside. Lifting my head up, I glanced at a clock on the wall. It was 12:15. I was about to head out another door that appeared to lead to a hallway when I saw another one to my side. There was a sign above it that read *The Honorable Judge Regina Duncan*. At that exact moment, the door opened suddenly opened and out walked Judge Regina Duncan, herself.

Instantly, our eyes locked.

After a couple seconds of tense silence, she raised a brow in recognition of me. Then she froze, like a store mannequin with her hand still grasping the doorknob as if undecided as to what to do next. She was dressed in civilian clothes, a beige blouse and a matching pencil skirt with brown three-inch heel pumps. In her other hand was a large briefcase that she was gripping hard enough to make her knuckles go white.

When I stroked the pistol in my right hand with my forefinger, contemplating whether or not I had the audacity to kill a Federal judge, she spoke. Her voice was calm like the gentle breeze that comes right before a violent storm; however, the pungency of her words were like claps of tumultuous thunder.

"This is foolish! You will never make it out of here! There are armed guards downstairs at the entrance lobby and, regardless of your clothes, everyone in here knows your face. You will be captured, possibly killed. You *will* fail," she said with conviction, just like how she'd delivered her verdict.

The cadence of her voice echoed as her eyes shifted, studying me intensely. She appeared calm, but I could see her fear hidden right underneath the surface of her demeanor in plain view. What she said was true, but there was one thing that she hadn't considered: her value to me.

"They will kill you."

"They're going to kill me anyways. I have you to thank for that."

"But you don't have to die *today*. You always have the chance to appeal again. But, if you do this, you'll never get the chance. You will die before they let you leave."

"Not if I take you with me," I responded and moved towards her.

Shocked, she chewed on her words like she had regurgitated her thoughts.

"I like my chances," I continued. "If I die, I am taking you with me. Almost like the death sentence you left me with. We can both die in a hailstorm of bullets and smoke, or you can help me get out of here and we both can live."

I saw her resolve shatter like broken glass on concrete as she leaned against the doorframe and sucked in a sharp breath. Releasing the doorknob, her hand reached for her chest and her shoulders slumped. I heard a noise coming from the door behind me; she must of heard it, too, because she cocked her head to the side as if listening.

"Let's go!" I said, sternly.

I was no stranger to danger, but what awaited my fate from that moment on… only God could have known. I didn't even know where the front door was, much less how to get out of the Federal building. There was only a matter of time before someone discovered that I was missing and, once that happened, a manhunt would ensue. I had to create some distance between me and this place, fast.

Surprisingly, the judge walked with ease as I guided her towards the front door. Her heels floated across the carpet as her posture changed. Like a chamberlain, she raised her chin with dignity. My judge-turned-hostage was fully cooperating. Then, suddenly, she stopped short just when we were about to walk out of the door and turned to look at me. I could see the wheels in her head turning as she observed every bit of my face. I knew that I had to look bad; my face was slightly bruised, and I had a limp.

"Here, take this and just walk with me. Try not to make eye contact with anyone. If I get you out of here safely, will you let me go?" she asked with an even tone. Reaching out, she handed me the heavy briefcase to hold.

I just stared at her a moment. Time was fragile, and I didn't have a lot of options. She must have read my thoughts.

"It's not uncommon for a bailiff or an attorney to help me out. This is normal, it can be used as a subterfuge to get us out."

I was grateful for her suggestion, but I didn't let it show. I needed to keep her fearful. Fearful hostages who were smart were more likely to cooperate.

"Subterfuge?" I blurted out as I took the briefcase and aimed the gun at her chest. "You better hope this shit works. If we don't make it out of here, I'm killing you first," I threatened and then placed the gun in my pocket.

She didn't even flinch, didn't beat an eye.

"There is blood on your face, and your eye is swollen. There are bruises." She pointed out.

Taking a moment, I wiped at the blood. There was nothing I could do about the swelling or the bruises.

"Did—did you hurt anyone? Are my bailiffs okay?" Her voice dipped an octave.

"Let's go," I said ignoring her question and glanced back up at the clock.

It was around lunchtime so, hopefully, the crowded corridor would aid me in my escape. I grabbed her elbow firmly and she inhaled a sharp breath.

When we walked out the door, the gravity of this new situation finally dawned on me.

Not only had I murdered two federal marshals and trapped four bailiffs in a room. Now, I had also just taken a United States Federal Judge as a hostage.

***

The corridor was congested with people galore as we shuffled along, with my hand holding the briefcase that I would quickly make into a weapon, if necessary. The .9 mm was in my pocket and the .44 caliber was stashed under my shirt, tucked firmly in the back.

As we moved, it seemed like everyone tried to stop and talk with the judge or ask her a question. My nerves began to unravel. She took notice and tried to ward off as many people as she could so that we could push on towards the exit. We were almost to the elevators when a white woman stopped her to ask about the court calendar. Instead of leaving right away, she then stated that she wanted to do lunch soon so that she could pick the judge's brain about law. As she spoke, she would occasionally smile and glance at me. Bowing my head, I cleared my throat and the judge abruptly ended the conversation.

By the time we made it to the elevator, just as it opened, it was packed with too many people, so we had to wait for the second one to arrive. I felt heat building at the base of my neck. For the first time, I considered whether or not I'd actually lost my mind.

"Judge Duncan!" a thick baritone called out with urgency.

The judge glanced over at my direction, lifting her hand slightly as if to tell me to chill, before turning around. I kept my head bowed but moved close enough to her to covertly press the barrel of my pistol into her back, reminding her that she could die at any time. Taking a quick look up at the approaching figure, I almost lost my shit.

The man wore a royal blue jacket with a crisp white shirt and tie. There was a military .45 strapped to his waist and a shiny badge on his chest. He was the sergeant bailiff. His hair was receding with a bald patch at the top and his skin was a brownish bronze with a sheen of perspiration on his forehead. For some reason, he was breathing hard. I noticed the walkie-talkie attached to his coat.

"Have you heard what is going on out in the streets, your Honor?" he asked as if he was agitated.

"No, what is it?" she responded. Miraculously, her tone seemed normal.

"After the episode that happened in your courtroom, several of the unruly gang members were arrested for inciting a riot. However, it didn't stop it from happening. Right now, there is a full-fledged riot going on in the streets right now. There are literally thousands of hoodlums, gang members tearing up the streets and everything around it. We are urging everyone to go to the café on the third floor for lunch instead of leaving the building and I put in a call to the police department to assist. It's crazy out there! Looks like a war zone."

"Whoa!" Judge Duncan replied.

Most likely her surprise was genuine. I was definitely shocked.

"Have you seen Brown, Smith or Clay or any of the bailiffs that work your courtroom? They aren't answering on the radio and I need their help immediately. I'm hoping they didn't already leave for lunch."

As he spoke, more and more people walked towards the elevator lobby. I grew impatient when I saw them all file on as soon as another elevator door opened, filling it immediately.

"No, I haven't," the judge replied. "They probably already left, Mr. Patton." She shrugged and then stole a glance at me.

With my body turned sideways and my hand on the banger in my pocket, I eased my other hand to the gun in the waist of my pants so that I could get off some clean shots in case any drama popped off.

"That is strange. I can't reach them or the federal marshals who brought Malik Shields to the hearing today in your courtroom. This is

LEO SULLIVAN

crazy, especially with all the chaos. The riots have caused all kinds of confusion down in inmate transportation, but something is not right about this." He scratched his bald head and glanced at me, then at the rest of the crowd.

My trigger finger moved instinctively; I was about to shoot him at pointblank range if he did anything to provoke me. I couldn't believe that The JDB were actually rioting in the streets but then again, this had been a long time coming. Bulletproof and Dolo were young and official with that social media shit. They'd been building up my support team for a while and, like the bonds that bound a gang, they used emotion to rally people to the cause. They created a national team of support for me by centering the focus on my good works and the things I did for my community. Many black people considered my case as another example of the white man trying to keep a black man down.

"This is despicable! I hope that is quelled with the help of law enforcement and that this thing gets resolved fast," the judge was saying.

Just then, another elevator opened. Fuck everything, this one I wouldn't miss.

"Judge, I think we need to hurry so I can help you and then assist the men outside."

Actually, if you don't mind assisting me in looking for her bailiffs and the marshals—"

"Excuse me! Excuse me!" I said, gripping the judge by the arm as I pushed by people to get through the elevator doors.

We squeezed on just in time, making extra room where there really was none left to take. We were packed in like sardines in a can. The judge and I stood chest-to-chest as the elevator descended. My heart was pounding, and my stomach was doing summersaults.

Duncan was looking up at me impassive, eyes locked into mine. Our bodies were pressed so tightly together; if I were a spoon, she would have been the liquid filling me. I fought the urge to turn away from the scornful expression on her face. Her unspoken anger felt as lethal as a hot burning sun.

Then the inevitable happened!

An alarm shrilled like a warning of a catastrophic event. It was the loudest noise I had ever heard and the lights in the elevator started to blink. I heard several disgruntled voices groan their discontent.

"The building is being placed on lockdown. They may know that you're trying to escape and whatever else you have done," she whispered in the crook of my neck. Her lips brushed across my chin and her breath was a Fahrenheit of guilt that threatened to consume me like an inferno from hell.

"Shit!" I hissed and furtively started easing the pistols out.

I was determined to shoot my way out of the building, if it came to that.

"No, don't do it!"

She seized my arm, but I pulled away. There was no way that I was going out without a fight and, if need be, I was taking her with me. Either give me liberty or give me death. One thing was for certain; I was not going back to that box in the supermax facility on death row.

The elevator dinged as it opened, and I clenched my jaw.

"Just trust me," she pleaded.

We piled out the elevator and there was commotion everywhere with cops and marshals scrambling around like they were running a drill.

"Everybody against the wall!" a voice hailed as several cops and deputy marshals moved in aggressively. I happened to glance out the window and, from a distance, I could see herds of young black people throwing objects and running wild. A car was on fire as well—it was pure pandemonium.

The judge took my arm and nudged me towards a metal detector with a slight nod of her head as police jostled about. An elderly white man with a mane of white hair, like the color of sheep's wool, stood in front of the metal detector as people rushed around. The deafening shrill from the alarm was still going off.

The elderly man raised his hand at Judge Duncan.

"We finna lock the building down, your Honor. I don't know why yet… maybe some type of attack or something. I can't let you out," he said, looking around with a grim face at all the sudden upheaval.

I glanced outside the window again and all I could see was a sea of angry brown faces, mostly juveniles, doing mayhem and destruction. What surprised me was a lot of them were women. I thought of Bulletproof and Dolo. This was their age group, and their fans. Their rebellious culture.

"I know, but me and my assistant have to get out of here before it gets worse. I have a flight to catch so that I can see my father. He is not doing well, as you know from when we spoke a while ago. I really need to go!" Her voice had an urgent demanding plea of authority to it.

Then, a mechanical voice came over the intercom.

"SECURE ALL ENTRANCES NOW! LOCK THEM DOWN. RIGHT NOW!"

As the voice blared, there were several people already at the door ahead of us about to exit and they continued to walk out without being hindered since the call had only just been issued.

"That alarm means we have a code red emergency. No one is to leave at this point," the old guy said with his head cocked to the side, observing the bedlam outside. "And it's not safe out there."

The judge took several steps closer to him with yet another desperate plea.

"I really need this favor. Please, just this once!" Her voice was stringent. The officer studied her for a second as I stood with my hand on the pistol in my pocket. Several officers were matching towards us from down the hall, their faces twisted with malicious purpose.

"Okay, y'all hurry. Since they just made the announcement and you're damn near at the door, just go. Be careful out there. They are mostly looting stores and attacking police cars, but I don't want you to be recognized as a judge."

"Thank you!" the judge said and took off.

I was right behind her with my hand in my pocket. I didn't like what I was seeing, there was too much commotion with cops and federal agents everywhere. An armored SWAT truck with a line of other military vehicles pulled up, and the men piled out single file, dressed in some type of black army fatigue. They each frowned, watching as waves of youth and young adults rushed by in hundreds, destroying vehicles, and throwing objects. It was crazy, and the police were outnumbered.

The streets were congested as the armed tactical unit moved about, but without control. Instead of suppressing the chaos, they were out of sync as they were all driven to protect themselves. Then, I suddenly heard a reverberating roar, like tumultuous thunder. I looked up in the sky, ensconced in an orange ball of luminous sun. There were police helicopters hovering ominously, so low I could make out the model of the AR-15 rifle that one of the cops was holding in his hand. He sat perched on the edge of the helicopter wearing some type of dark helmet with bug-eyed glasses. The assault rifle in his hands was aimed down at the streets which were teeming with people, as he spoke into some type of radio apparatus that was attached to his helmet. I knew that though he was watching the riot below, they weren't his target. He was looking for me.

I lassoed my arm around the judge's shoulders, pulling her tight so she could feel the gun in my pocket, subconsciously reminding her that she was still in danger.

"Where is your car parked?" I asked, walking briskly in herds of people. It was perfect camouflage.

She nodded with her head towards the parking garage just as several masked SWAT team members rushed in. They were heavily armed, wearing helmets, body shields, and followed by some type of armored vehicle like the ones I had seen in the military.

"We can't go in there," I said under my breath.

Taking her arm, I inconspicuously lead her through throngs of youth, then across a busy street into traffic as people bumped into us. She stumbled but managed to keep her balance in her pump heels as I towed her with me, determined to escape.

"Where we going? You said you would let me go!" she shouted above the roar of noise; her face was suddenly panic-stricken.

"Right, I am going to let you go when we get out. We still in the middle of a war zone."

My mind was frantically searching for a way out. It was matter of time before an all-points bulletin would be placed out on me with a picture, possibly the judge, too. With all the modern technology, I was certain that there was going to be a video of me up adducting the judge from the building and walking out the courthouse.

The thing was, I didn't have a set plan, didn't have any idea of how to escape. I was moving on instinct and fueled by the adrenaline rushing through my veins. All of my moves were by happenstance and blind, like a precarious destiny of walking across a path full of hungry lions. I couldn't stumble or fall. I had to distance myself from the courthouse by any means necessary.

As we walked with people rushing by, I heard a gunshot. Suddenly, there was an explosion, a large canister sailed past my foot. There was smoke coming out of the fuse and my eyes began to burn along with my throat and nose. It was teargas. My mind formulated a plan and it was risky as fuck. As I took the judge's hand and moved even faster, a store shop window suddenly exploded. Rioters ran inside in droves as the police just looked on in horror.

As soon as we turned the corner, I spotted a guy seated in a black Infinity, he was talking urgently on his phone. Directly across from him were looters, busy burning a car. In front of him was a homeless person leaning against the wall at awe. The homeless guy appeared to be mentally disturbed; he was moving his hands all animated like he was engaged in a conversation with an invisible person in a heated argument. His dark skin was a swarthy-black and dirty. His clothes were tattered and filthy; they looked old enough to date back to the Jesus era. In fact, so did he, but he could serve a purpose in my escape plan.

"Wait right here," I ordered the judge and pulled out my pistol. She flinched, like I was going to shoot her. My intent was to let her know that if she did attempt to run, then she would be shot.

I marched up to the guy in the Infinity and eased the passenger door open before sliding in next to him and pressing the gun against his ribcage. He looked up, startled. He had been so engrossed in sending a text on his cellphone that he hadn't noticed me approaching until it was too late.

"Give me the phone," I demanded.

Instead of moving, he hesitated, as if weighing his options.

"This is a robbery. Don't make it a murder," I said evenly as I established eye contact. I lifted the gun to let him know that I was fully intent on pushing his wig back.

"Hey, buddy, take whatever you want. Just don't kill me. I have a wife and children."

"Get the fuck out the car and leave the keys. Then go stand over there next to my partner over there wrapped in that blanket. He's hiding a bomb and if you try to walk away, he is going to detonate it and blow this place to smithereens," I said, nudging my head towards the homeless man. Appearing crazy as ever, he was still in a heated argument with himself.

The white guy nodded his head and hopped out of the car to do exactly what I'd said. The homeless man stopped talking to stare hard at the other man. With his dirty fist lifted, he hauled off and punched the white man hard, yelling that he was standing too close. Something about their quick altercation incited the passing rioters and they joined in, kicking the white man in the stomach and head. This was insane; I had never seen anything like this. It was like the end of days.

I stole a glance at the judge. She was nervous, jittery even, as her eyes darted around. I could tell she was thinking about making a run until her eyes settled on me.

Once I started the car, I waved for her to come over and, again, she looked around with devastation showing clear in her eyes before she complied. She ambled over in a fog of smoke and I eased down the window, watching her mop at the tuft of hair on her forehead as a whist of wind pushed her it all over her face. She held her hand to her mouth and her eyes were red and puffy from the tear gas.

"I didn't kill those people in the house or molest that child. I was framed," I said, putting the car in gear. It was going to be a problem trying to maneuver around all the herds of people.

"I know you didn't do it," she said, shocking me with her admission.

"Well, why didn't you rule in my favor?" I raised my voice but tried to maintain my control.

Taking a glance behind her, she then responded, "Politics. It's election season and I couldn't risk being seen as lenient on violent crime. I hated the decision that I had to make, but I was positive that you would have been released once granted another appeal."

"An appeal that could have taken five or ten years," I clarified.

She shrugged. "Better than a death sentence."

I rubbed at my eyes, just about to drive off when suddenly the loud, reverberating sound of a helicopter echoed in my ears from up ahead. And then my worst fear became a reality when I looked up and saw a cop on a loudspeaker peering down, directly at me.

"MALIK SHIELDS, STEP OUT OF THE CAR WITH YOUR HANDS UP!"

Fuck.

I grimaced and looked down at the guns in my hands. This couldn't be the way I let things end.

Reaching out the window, I snatched the judge by the neck and pushed the barrel of my pistol against her dome. She screamed bloody murder and tried to fight me. Sadly, I had just been about to let her go, but that was no longer an option.

Holding her closely, I used her as a barrier between myself and the helicopter and headed towards a parking deck located adjacent to where we stood.

"Hey, that's King!" I heard somebody yell, followed by the repetition of other voices saying the same thing.

Luck was on my side yet again when the crowd of looters then turned their attention to the helicopter and began tossing various objects at the officer. Someone, most likely the person setting the police squad cars on fire, tossed a Molotov cocktail and I heard the officer begin to panic, urging his pilot to fall back. I took advantage of the quick diversion and released the judge to flee into the parking deck before rushing into another building nearby, hoping that I would throw off the police on foot once they came after me.

It didn't take long before I reached a dead end; an alley with a single door at the end. I tried it, but it was locked. Pricking my ears, I picked up on the sound of shuffling feet coming from the same area that I'd just been in. The police were closing in. Looking fast, I saw a small door a few yards ahead from where I stood and I ran up to try it, praying that the door would give. It did, but I groaned when I saw that it was only a small outdoor closet. With no other option available and the people tracking me closing in, I dove inside.

"He's over here," someone outside said. "I saw him. Try that door."

Sucking in a breath, I clutched both of my guns and positioned my finger on the triggers.

The door then burst open and, before I knew it, I was looking down the barrel of a gun. With my finger still on the trigger of the weapons in my hand, I was already aiming and prepared to shoot when something made me pause.

"SHIT! King, what da fuck? Nigga, I almost shot you!"

Never before had I been so happy to see another man in my life. Bulletproof lowered the pistol in his hand and stepped to the side to reveal Dolo who was standing next to him.

"Damn, you put in work! They been talkin' 'bout them bodies you left at the courthouse. You on the radio and the news," he marveled for a brief second, a look of admiration on his face.

I was so dumbfounded; I couldn't even speak.

"We gotta get out of here now," Bulletproof said and took a glance behind him. "The hood is rioting for you hard, creating the distraction we needed to get you out of here, but the SWAT has really moved in. We don't have a lot of time."

That was all I needed to hear. They'd brought me a weapon much better than what I had on me, so I dropped the Glocks in my hand and exchanged them for the AK-47 that Dolo was holding out to me. Once we stepped out, taking a side street, it took me a couple seconds to adjust to more chaos outside. It was pure pandemonium. Masses of black people—my people—were still running around wrecking shit in every way they could. They were relentless, propelled by their unified goal.

The armed security and bailiffs were using batons, tasers and pepper spray to try to control the crowd but there were too many of them. I knew that there was only a matter of time before firepower became their next method of choice and I hoped to be long gone before that shit got started. If necessary, I wouldn't hesitate to bust shots, but I didn't want it to come to that. As it turned out, it wouldn't. The moment we got a few steps out the door, about five other men, all JDBs, surrounded me with their weapons in the air.

"Gunner is around back with the getaway car ready to go. Let's move!" Bulletproof shouted out and everyone began to move. They created a shield around me to the point that I couldn't see shit, but I could hear it all.

"Jo... behind you!"

The next second I heard shots fired, coming from Jo's weapon as he gunned someone down. The team of men didn't miss a beat. They ushered me out of a back alley and the second the bright sunlight hit my eyes, I felt a joyous feeling erupt in my chest.

"There he is! Get King inside!" Bulletproof gave the order and in the next moment, I was being pushed inside of an open door in the back of a Brinks truck. Once I was inside, the men took off in opposite directions, heading toward other vehicles to make their escape.

"Welcome back, King," was the last thing Dolo said to me before he smiled, gave me a quick salute, and then slammed the door closed.

"Welcome back, boss," another person said. I looked up and was relieved to see my nigga, Gunner, sitting in the driver's seat.

"I'm happy as hell to see you, bruh," I told him as he took off driving away from the courthouse.

A simple nod was his response before he placed his full attention on the road, driving carefully and attentively to our next destination. The other members of The JDBs had us surrounded, making sure that we didn't run into trouble.

Falling back, I let out a deep, long and much needed breath and then closed my eyes. It hadn't happened like I wanted it to, but Malik 'King' Shields was finally free.

As soon as that thought sunk in, another one crossed my mind. I couldn't push away my desire to see Sunday. She was laid up in a hospital bed, not too far away, fighting for her life. If something happened and I missed the chance to see her, I would never forgive myself. I had to be near her. It was crazy, reckless and stupid, but I loved her.

Chapter Nine
~
Sunday

Sometime during the night, Kelly and my mama left to get some rest before what my doctor told them would be a long and difficult next few days. Once my baby was born, they would not only be watching me fight for my life, but they'd have to watch his fight as well. I found myself floating in and out of some unexplainable state of consciousness. I was in limbo, caught somewhere between life and death. Sometimes I didn't know what was real and what was fake. It all felt like a dream.

My senses jolted when I became aware of my room door opening and a hum of sounds coming from the hospital corridor rushed in. Once the door closed, there was silence, with only the muffled sound of the machines that were keeping me alive churning. In my head, my aching heart was palpitating with a rhythm of its own. Suddenly, I smelled a scent—a manly scent that my body immediately responded to like when a woman knows her man is near. I inhaled him deeply through my nostrils and his intoxicating, invigorating and manly musk entered my soul, impaling my mind with lust, love and all kinds of emotions I was at a loss to explain.

I could feel his breath on my cheek and the fine hairs on his chin brushing against my neck. He was watching me; I could feel his eyes on my body, dancing along my skin. He observed me closely but there was nothing eerie or creepy about this moment. Somehow, I felt like I was in the presence of someone who loved me deeply. My soulmate, someone who had given me his heart.

Is this Caesar?

Though the thought occurred to me, something told me that it wasn't.

I was in a pleasant state, like a blissful dream, and the moment was so tender and peaceful, I wondered if I were actually in a dream. It felt so real but yet, I wasn't sure. But then he spoke, and I knew without a shadow of a doubt that I was definitely dreaming. Even still, at the sound of his voice, my heart melted.

"Sunday... I don't know if you can hear me but I'm sorry. I never meant for it to be like this..."

He choked up and buried his face in the crook of my neck. I felt my heart beating a hundred beats a minute. The dream felt so real.

"I... I don't know what happened. I don't know what went wrong but, Sunday, I ain't have nothing to do with this or the shit that got me locked up. I promise you one thing, I'ma find out who did it. I would never let anyone do some shit like this to you... to your baby... and get away with it. A bunch of niggas 'bout to get eternal dirt naps over this. I put my life on that. I would lay my life down for you."

I felt his lips on my skin and they felt so real, just like I remembered in the days when I felt them on my skin every day. My emotions built and I felt tears come to my eyes. In that moment, I was reminded of just how much I missed King. I would always love him.

"Until the day that God takes the last breath from my body, I'll love you, Sunday. No matter what, Malik 'King' Shields will always love you. If you forget everything else, don't ever forget that."

The sound of footsteps walking away was the last thing I heard before the door opened and shut once again. Although I couldn't see him leave, I could feel the absence of his presence in the room. Disappointment flooded my consciousness as I realized that, once again, I was alone.

Many hours later, I remember being pushed into a room with more bright lights and I could hear the shuffle of feet. People were laughing and joking; the room was cold and damp. The pleasant dream I'd had was now a distant memory as I was pulled back into my half-reality where the murmuring of hospital personnel, beeping machines and devastating hopelessness in regard to my current state, reigned supreme.

"No need to give her an epidural for the pain. She is in a coma, so she won't feel a thing. No moving or complaints. Let's pop this baby out and get to lunch. This is easy money."

If I could've cringed, I would have. Better yet, I would have jumped right off the table.

They are about to deliver my baby! I thought, remembering what my doctor had said the day before.

I should have been excited about the moment, but I was terrified. That horror was only magnified by the facetious and callous conversations happening around me.

They all laughed and chatted like it was just another day on the job, but I could hear everything. I felt hands on my body; something rubbed against my stomach, wet liquid, it was cold and sticky. Then a sharp, splitting cut, from one side of my belly to the other. The pain came next—more pain than I had ever experienced in my life, but yet I couldn't move, couldn't resist, couldn't scream. Either they had given me some medication that had finally taken hold, or my mind was able to block out the majority of the pain because it finally began to subside.

However, I could still feel the pulling and tugging. I felt hands inside of me probing, pulling, jerking, and then, next, a whoosh. There was a snapping sound that scorched through my body.

The hands left and there was a smacking sound right before I heard the most beautiful, dulcet sound in the world: a baby crying. It was my baby. His cries grew louder, tugging at my maternal instincts and somehow in all the inertia of pain and oblivion, I found my way back to life.

It was like a weight lifted from me, like I was suddenly freed from being bound in chains. I awoke with a start. The bright lights electrocuted stung my eye.

"Holy shit!" someone said, taking a step back.

"What the f—" another voice was about to say.

"Gimme… my… baby," I croaked with a dry mouth. My tongue felt like sandpaper as the lights set my one good eye ablaze.

"Ms. Kennedy! What a pleasure to have you back."

I looked up into the haze of lights and saw a beautiful young black woman about my age. She had an afro covered with a hospital sanitation garb; her eyes embraced me with a smile. I tried to return the greeting with a smile of my own, but I felt drunk, woozy, like I was floating in and out of consciousness. Hands were all over my body as my vitals and other things were checked. In the far corner, the pediatric staff was tending to my baby and I wanted to call out for them to hand him to me, but I couldn't.

"I see you're awake," someone above me was saying. "Just stay calm. We are tending to you and your baby. You both will be fine."

It was my doctor talking. I was so familiar with his voice, but I had never seen him until now. His skin was white as snow and he had a mane of brunette hair. I could tell that, back in his day, he was a woman charmer. Suddenly, I winced. The bright lights were sending shock waves of pain through my head.

He must have misunderstood my expression.

"Oh, by the way, I'm Dr. Stevens."

"I... know who... you ... are..." I minced my words terribly as I squinted, my eyes trying to adjust to the blaring lights.

"Okay. Can you move your arms?" he asked as the hospital staff just stood around gawking at me in awe.

At the time I didn't know that it was because I wasn't supposed to have made it this far. They thought that if I did survive, I would be comatose and brain dead. I guess no one ever told them about Mama's prayers or the power of God.

I purposely ignored his request. My baby was crying like he was being tortured.

"Let me see my baby!" I managed to say.

"Nurse Beverly, when it's safe to do so, can you please bring the baby over?" Dr. Stevens said while still looking at me like I had performed some miraculous feat.

Moments later, a bundle of joy, still crying was placed on my chest and I received the shock of my life.

"This... this is my baby?" I asked, feeling fresh tears come to my eyes.

"Yes," Dr. Stevens replied with a wide smile. "This is your baby girl."

Lowering my head, I kissed my daughter on her forehead, feeling a kind of love that I'd never felt before.

A girl?

I couldn't believe it. I had been told that I was having a boy. How could this be that for all this time, my doctors had gotten it wrong?

I had so many tubes and contraptions hooked up to my body and I had also been lying motionless for so long that my limbs could barely move. With the help of the nurse, I was able to hold my baby and the moment that she was settled in my arms, she stopped crying and started to coo. I smiled when she looked at me with eyes that looked exactly like mine, but then I frowned suddenly. I picked on some type of gurgling sound, like she was having trouble breathing. Her frail body looked emaciated and weak. She was born premature, a month early, and I had lost a lot of blood prior to her birth. It was a miracle that she was alive. We had been through so much; we were both lucky to be here.

"Oh, shit! You're awake. Sunday, you're awake!"

Hearing the familiar voice, I turned my head with a little difficulty. It felt like my neck had a crook in it from lying in the same position for so long.

"Caesar!" I croaked as my eyes adjusted to the light and his beautiful hue.

"They brought me to see the baby being born. I was outside until they just let me in. I wasn't expecting to see you."

He tried to smile but I saw his wounded façade underneath as a nurse stood behind his wheelchair. For a fleeting second, I thought I saw him frown and flinch a little when he looked at me. I knew I was probably horrifically scarred and there was no telling what my eye looked like.

"I just thank God that you and the baby are okay. Can I hold him?"

"Her," I corrected him with a smile. "We had a girl."

His jaw dropped in shock. "What? Oh shit!"

Caesar's face was all black and blue and he had a huge gauze on his head. It almost looked like a turban as he tried to smile but his eyes wouldn't comply. They were dark and somber like there was a dim light coming from his spirit.

"Here," was all I could muster, my voice was hoarse.

"She... she has your eyes," Caesar said as he held his hands out for her.

Taking her into his arms, he pulled her close to his chest and something about that moment touched me. Before I knew it, I had started crying. If there was ever such a thing as a miracle, we were the testament to it. The entire staff looked on, and then one person started clapping. Before long, all the others had joined in.

"What are all you clapping for? This ain't no fuckin' celebration, this is a muthafuckin' devastation. We almost died!" Caesar raged.

"Bae... No, don't do that."

"No, what? I may be paralyzed for life. I'm wearing a fuckin' shit bag and I'm only twenty-six years old. And look at you and the baby. What have we done to deserve this? Then here they go, fuckin' clapping. We don't need your fuckin' sympathy!"

The black nurse spoke up, her mascara was ruined from crying.

"It wasn't about sympathy. We're just happy for you and your family that's all." She wiped at a tear in her eye.

"Thank you," I said and reached for Caesar to calm him.

I could only imagine what he was going through, but this wasn't the way to deal with it by taking his frustration out on innocent people. Reaching out, I ran my finger along the side of our child's face, appreciating her beauty. Once again, I thought I saw Caesar glance at me, and a shadow of a frown passed over his face before he looked away.

As he held his daughter and caressed her little hand with one delicate finger, all I could do was try to hold back tears. I needed to be strong for both of them.

"You're probably going to need plastic surgery to fix your face. I'ma have to get outta here and get some money for us soon. I felt a tingling in my legs, and I know that means I'ma walk again—"

"Plastic surgery? My... face?"

His words cut me to the core. Did I really look that bad? I was briefly reminded of the dream that I had with King coming into my room, kissing my face, and telling me that I was beautiful. Or to be precise, *still* beautiful. Until this moment, I hadn't once thought about my appearance, but King had mentioned it. Was that really a dream?

"Wh—what's wr-wr-wrong with my face?"

The words came out jumbled and scattered, like marbles tossed across a wooden floor.

"I'm just saying, you gon' need to get it fixed... But I'll get money for that."

My animus was getting the better of me. Something about him started to annoy me. Maybe it was the way he was looking at me like I repulsed him—a direct contrast from the tender loving kisses I'd received in my dream.

"You needing money is what got us here in the *first* place, Caesar."

"No, what got us in here was King. He set that entire jack move up."

Instantly, I felt my finger clutch the sheet. Here he was bringing up King's name again but with good reason this time. As much as I wanted to lash out and respond, I fought to keep my mouth shut. Until the night before, I believed the same thing that he did, but it didn't seem right anymore.

"Ms. Kennedy, we are going to take the baby to the NICU and get you to your room so you can rest up. I've already given you something in your I.V. to help you sleep. After a few hours, the doctor will come to perform some tests."

"I've already slept enough..." I remember mumbling before whatever medication they'd given me began to take over.

Before I could stop it, I drifted off, praying that my child would be okay. Caesar's words hurt so badly that I had terrible dreams about my eyeball sinking into my face, looking like a deep gaping hole. In the dream, I was so hideous that he eventually left me for another woman.

Chapter Ten

Sunday

When I awoke, my mind was all over the place. There was a room full of people, my mother, a few of her friends and co-workers, Caesar, Kelly and even the police. It was like a madhouse, but the only thing that mattered to me was my baby.

"Where is she?" I managed to ask. For some reason, my throat was dry, and my eyes burned.

"She is still in intensive care. I will ask the nurse if they can bring you to her in a minute. She is a fighter," my mom said with melancholy and took my hand.

Everyone else in the room had turned and was staring at me at awe. Like they knew something I didn't. I would soon find out.

A plainly dressed cop with a huge bulbous nose, ruddy cheeks, platinum hair came forward and introduced himself as Detective Wilmer.

"Your ex-boyfriend, Malik Shields killed two government workers, kidnapped a federal judge and escaped from a high security federal building today. We have reason to believe that he is or was in this hospital. One of the staff here says that your brother, a man that matched his description, was given permission to come to your room. Did you see him? Your life could be in grave danger."

"I—I don't have a brother," was all that I was able to say.

My mind then reflected on what I'd thought was a dream and I stirred. The officer eyed me suspiciously before moving on.

"Well, we don't know much other than that, but we are still searching the hospital and we'll keep an officer stationed outside," the cop replied.

I sat up in bed with cinematic flashes of King kissing my face. I could almost smell the scent of his body on mine and feel my emotions stirring as his dulcet words penetrated my heart. It all had seemed so real, so true. It was beautiful.

"Officer, I told you if he was in the building, he never made it to her room. I would have never allowed it," Caesar said as he rolled his wheelchair closer. The officer lifted a brow and took a long look at Caesar, as if suggesting that there wasn't much that he could do in his current position.

"Plus," Caesar added. "If he would have been here, we would both be dead. From what I've seen, that nigga on a killing spree."

"I have to agree, if the culprit would have been here, there would probably been violence. There has been a massive manhunt for him since it was discovered that he had escaped, so I doubt he would have taken the risk to come here, anyways. But, to be on the safe side, we are placing twenty-four-hour security outside the door and downstairs in the corridor. An extra measure of safety."

"You all should have already done that," someone said.

****

Once the cop and the others in my room left, I was taken to see my baby girl for a brief moment, just enough time to feed her. When I returned to my room, Kelly was perched in a chair, tapping away on a brand-new iPhone. Across from her, Caesar was on the opposite side of the room, looking up at television. Judging from the expression on his face, he was enthralled with something fascinating. After the nurse and my mama helped me back into the bed, I glanced up at the television and gasped.

It looked like an inferno with cars and shops burning as masses of people ran back and forth through the streets. The scene reminded me of something that would only happen in a war-torn, third-world country. It couldn't be real.

"What is going on? Is that the city burning? That looks like downtown Atlanta. Are they shooting a movie?"

"Not a movie," Kelly lifted her head to answer me. "They sayin' that's King and his John Doe Boys. They started a riot to help him escape. They out there robbin' and lootin' stores. I already hit up a few of my girls and asked them to pick me up some shit."

My jaw dropped as I watched the scene unfolding in front of me like clips from a movie. There was no way that King was a part of this. I took in the details reluctantly, swallowing hard as every word the reporter said sunk in. People had been murdered, hurt and beaten behind what he did. I watched as people screamed and cried tears as officers sprayed them directly in the face with pepper spray and tear gas. Billows of smoke erupted from cars that had been set on fire; people dove for cover and others, officers and civilians alike, tried to run.

"I don't believe it," I whispered, watching with tears in my eyes. "There was no way that King could have been behind all this."

"I keep tellin' you that you don't know that nigga like you think you do," Caesar piped up while popping a pill into his mouth. He'd been taking his pain pills like candy.

"He's dangerous, crazy and he is tryin' to kill every muthafucka who is responsible for gettin' him locked up. The next person he'll be comin' after is you. But, don't worry, I got you," he added, cutting his eyes towards me. "We gon' get you fixed up and then get through this together."

"What are you going to do?" I raised my voice a falsetto of fear. I didn't want to point out the obvious; he was in a wheelchair, but even without it, he'd never been a match for King.

"My legs already workin' again and they gonna get stronger. I got this. I'ma handle mine."

"What?" I shook my head. "We have a baby to think about. Haven't you had enough of the violence? If people are tryin' to kill us, wouldn't it make sense for us to take our baby and move away?"

"Da fuck? So, I'm 'posed to be a coward? Run, 'cause I'm scared of King?" he asked giving me a blank stare then looked away.

Our silence hummed like a thief stealing borrowed time. I felt so alone, like no one understood how I felt. Not even the one person who should have. Since our ordeal, Caesar hadn't once hugged me or shown any bit of affection. He was just callous, appearing to have no empathy.

"Caesar, do you still love... me?"

My voice trembled.

He swallowed hard and I watched as his Adam's apple bobbed. Then he slowly turned and looked at me, pausing for a moment. When he looked into my face, he grimaced, and I felt ugly and dirty.

"Sunday, a lot has happened... To be honest, I don't know no more," he replied with a subtle shrug.

Turning his back to me, he looked away. That time, he didn't look at the television, but out the window, as a billow of smoke rose like gray haze, enveloping the city.

Chapter Eleven
~ Sunday ~

"I'm ugly now. Look at my face! That's why Caesar don't love me anymore. Maybe I should have died."

"Fuck him! All he wanna do these days is pop pills. He stay high off them percs that the doctor gave him. Who cares what he thinks? Plus, you're good, girl," Kelly jumped in while scrolling on her phone.

My mama sucked her teeth at Kelly's choice of words.

A tear ran down my cheek as I looked in the hand mirror that my mama had given me. There was a gash on the right side of my head with sixteen stitches; it was a grisly, horrific scar. My eye was closed and swollen black and blue due to the impact of the bullet. Because of the pressure placed on my brain from the trauma of the bullet, I couldn't see out my right eye. The doctor had warned me that there was a possibility that I could permanently lose my vision, lose my eye, have to get surgery or even possibly a prosthetic eye, in the worst-case scenario.

Before I could stop myself, I threw the mirror on the floor, smashing it.

"Now why did you do that? You're wrong. You're still very beautiful and Caesar loves you. We spoke; he is just going through a lot, he is young and stressed out, too. At first, they said he could run the chance of being paralyzed but, recently with therapy, he has been making great progress. You gon' to have to work with him and be patient," my mama said.

"Mama, I don't wanna live like that... walking on eggshells. He don't love me."

The right side of my face was grotesquely disfigured badly and enlarged. The first image that came to mind when I looked at my reflection was of Emmitt Till's terribly beaten body. Caesar's words were still fresh in my head.

"Don't say that. Plus, now you just broke that mirror. You're trying your luck," Kelly said, nodding her head, animated. Her eyes were red and slanted. She had been smoking weed and was high as usual.

My mama grabbed my hand and squeezed it. "Never say such bad things like that. You're still a beautiful girl. Never judge your value by the exterior, it's the interior that counts the most. Never forget that," she said, causing a smile to tug at the corners of her mouth. However, her eyes were sad.

All I could do was just stare at her and watch the bundle of her pent-up love and devotion for me, her only child, as tears streamed down my face.

"I have to talk to you about something, Sunday."

The medication was strong; I was fighting sleep. Whatever the nurse had been placing in the I.V. bottle for pain was doing its job. I actually nodded twice, falling asleep and woke up drooling with my mouth wide open.

"They're going to have to perform surgery on the baby. One of the valves in her heart is not working properly and she is having issues with her kidneys and liver. It's basically a host of things."

My spirits sunk farther; the baby was the only bright spot in my life at that point. She was in the NICU in critical condition and, needless to say, we were all extremely concerned. I needed to take my baby home with me.

Kelly got up, walked over and held my hand; she smelled just like loud and perfume. We had been friends for years. She moved to Atlanta from Baltimore with her alcoholic druggy mother along with three younger sisters and a baby brother around seven. Men found her strikingly gorgeous in that urban hood type of way. She had a caramel complexion with long wavy natural back hair that cascaded down to her butt and made you want to question her ethnicity. She had large perky breasts and a very curvy figure with a big butt and dazzling smile that she used to her advantage to seduce guys with the wiles of her charm. She resembled a young version of Lisa Raye in her best days.

"I'm going to go check on the baby. Caesar has been up there all morning," my mama said. She kissed me on my wet cheek and exited the room just as I was going off into another drug induced nod.

As soon as she was gone, Kelly walked closer. Suddenly, she was filled with jubilance as she caressed my hair affectionally before standing back to fully get my attention.

"I need to talk you about something that could possibly cheer you up," Kelly said and pushed a tuft of hair off her forehead.

For the first time in my life, I felt a twinge of jealousy for another woman's beauty. I was always one of the most attractive women in a room, but things were about to change drastically.

"There is nothing you could tell me that would possibly cheer me up. My baby is fighting for her life!" I said, steeped in misery and allowing anger to consume me capriciously.

"The baby is going to be well and you too. You just can't give up hope. It's that medication kicking your ass—got you thinking Caesar hatin' on you. I was just kiddin' 'bout what I said earlier, that nigga loves your dirty drawers. You wanna smoke something? It will make you feel better." Kelly had a sparkling of mischief in her eyes as she dipped her hand in her knock-off Versace purse.

"No," I responded flatly and then turned my head away from her as another tear slid down my check. "I wanna go upstairs to be with my baby." I mournfully pulled the sheets up to my chin as more tears slid down my face. I couldn't help it.

"I know, but the doctor said you would be in no condition to be moved or else I would have placed you in a wheelchair and took you up there. As it is now, you can hardly keep your eyes open. Besides, you just pushed out a whole big ass baby." She chuckled before reaching out to take my hand.

"I know... but... I hate... this so much!" I complained, nearly drifting off to sleep.

"Hold on though, peep this: I was talking to this guy named Shawn. He is like the weed man and he's big time. He drives a brand-new BMW, wears designer clothes with a lot of drip and his jewelry game is tight as fuck! Anyways, he likes me," she said, all hype and all I could do was roll my eyes at her. I already knew that if he liked her and he was the weed man and he was paid, that he had definitely contributed to her habit of smoking weed all day, every day.

"So, what are you saying?" I was groggy as I raised my voice and my hand absentmindedly grasped the sheet to squeeze it tight. I was doing my best not to fall back asleep, and I was growing angrier by the second as I turned and looked at her.

"So, anyways, Shawn is related to these guys who sell major weight: coke, mollies, loud, syrup and all that. Daze and his crew associates with them—"

"Daze!" I perked up as my heart began to pound in my chest.

"Yep." She gave me a devious grin.

"I told you what he did... he was the one who raped me. He was part of the group who tried to kill all of us," I said with a shudder.

"That's what I'm tryin' to explain to you. Let me finish!" Kelly shot her arms up in the air and rolled her eyes like I was getting on her nerves. "Shawn works with them, smuggling drugs for some organization. There is a stash at this club they all go to party at and he said it has more than twenty-five million dollars in it. Daze is part of the crew, him and all his friends hang out there. They are all in some type of gang with rappers and entertainers in it. They fuck with Future also; I saw it all on their Instagram."

"So what are you telling me for? I just want them all dead."

"Bitch, right! That's why I'm telling you. This is our chance to get revenge, to get their ass. You couldn't ask for a better situation."

"Not really, because I don't do stuff like that," I said, annoyed and disgusted that Kelly would even try me like that.

As it was, I was catching hell with my baby not doing well and fiancé possibly being paralyzed. If I had it my way, I would have just snitched to the police and told them all about Daze, but in the hood where I'm from, that would have only gotten us killed.

"This is the perfect situation, and this is a blessing in disguise because karma gon' get them niggas. They gon' end up dead or in jail and you ain't goin' to get shit out of it but more media. In the news, all they talking about is how you was raped, shot and left for dead while pregnant. People have been keepin' up with this story like a soap opera."

"Umm, please! I don't want to talk about it no more," I said drowsier than ever.

I remember Kelly sending words at me in rapid fire, nonstop talking. I dozed off twice, fighting sleep. Annoyed about it all, I slid down in bed, discouraged. She had a point; the media had been in a frenzy and although it made national news, I had not received one dime. People were asking me for statements, interviews and all but, at the end of the day, I was still broke, my face was fucked up and my child was fighting for her life.

"Just trust me Sunday. You don't have to do shit. I'll show you how to rock these niggas to sleep, B-More style. They won't even know what hit 'em," she said and reached into her purse. When she pulled out a baby Glock .9 mm and placed her hand on her curvy hip, I watched as she leaned forward with an expression on her face that I knew all too well.

"Wh—where you get that gun from?" I asked, feeling slightly afraid. It wasn't like I hadn't been around guns before but after being shot and almost killed, that was the last thing I wanted to see. Maybe I was suffering from a mild case of PTSD.

"I stay strapped, especially after the shit that you went through. I ain't playin' around, and if somebody come up in here to finish off what they started with you, I'ma have something waiting for them," she replied, sucking her teeth as she fingered the barrel of the gun.

Being from Baltimore, Kelly moved a lot faster than chicks in Atlanta. She grew up in Cherry Hill in Bean Town. The city had a high crime rate and either you got killed or learned how not to at an early age. She once told me about how she shot two boys when she was fifteen years old for messing with her little sister. Neither of them died, but that was a lot for me.

"Shawn is lame as fuck so I know I can spin him how I wants. He doesn't even know who I am and been bragging to me about the club and how him and Daze's crew be hanging out, drinking and counting money. I ain't even given him any pussy yet with his musky-Moose-breath-having ass."

She stopped and giggled at her own corny joke.

"I don't want nothing to do with that and you need to stay out of it, too," I told her.

"Do you think that King had something to do with it?" Kelly suddenly asked. "The word on the streets is that he never forgave you for leaving him when he was down. You moved on with Caesar, got pregnant, and left Makita's hoe-ass to hold him down."

The second she mentioned King, my heart ached. I didn't want to believe that he was behind the attack on my life, but I also couldn't deny that I'd betrayed him. Though I never meant to fall for Caesar, definitely didn't plan on having a baby with him, the fact still remained that when he needed me most, I wasn't around. When all of the mounting evidence came out, I knew in my heart that he wasn't guilty, however, rumors began to circulate that he'd moved on with Makita while he was locked up.

One day, I went to the prison to visit him and that was the day he broke my heart. Due to me being initially charged with the murders because of the police finding me with the dead bodies, King asked me to visit him under his roomie's name instead of his so the record wouldn't show me coming to see him and I wouldn't get inadvertently mixed up in his case. He had an agreement with his bunkmate so that when he knew I was coming, he would take the visit on his roommate's behalf.

On this particular day, I didn't get a chance to tell him I was coming prior to my visit because it wasn't planned. I'd just been evicted from our apartment and, in an act of desperation, I was going to see King to ask for some kind of help or advice on what to do next. When I arrived, what I didn't know was that he was already on a visit. I walked into the visitation room and was greeted with the sight of him tongue-kissing Makita like she was his new bride. That day, I left and never returned. It was also the day that I decided to move on with my life.

"Please, put that gun up," I spoke in a small voice, feeling weak as my medication began to take hold. "I don't want to see it anymore."

"Oh," she looked at the gun in her hand with a sheepish expression on her face before looking back up at me. "Yeah, I guess I should've thought better about bringin' this in here after everything you went through."

I nodded and then closed my eyes just as she finished her sentence. Before I knew it, I was dosing off to sleep again. It was the end for me; the drugs were too powerful. What they had me on was as powerful as a horse tranquilizer and knocked me out cold. Vaguely, I could hear Kelly calling my name, but I was too far gone. I was in a utopia, a dream type state, at peace with the world.

When I finally drifted off, it was into a peaceful sleep. Like so many times before, especially in the days leading up to that one, I dreamed about King.

Chapter Twelve
~
Sunday

Three months later

"Surprise! Home, sweet home!"

With a weak smile on my face, I turned away from the broad grin on Kelly's face and fixed my eyes on the group of people standing in the room in front of me with their arms spread wide. They were waiting for me to respond with... something, I didn't know. Excitement, most likely, but I was too overwhelmed to make it seem genuine.

"Thank you," I replied, dropping my head to shield my face.

Though a few months had passed since the incident that landed me in the hospital and I was healing well from the plastic surgery I'd gotten to repair the damage to my face, I still felt self-conscious about my looks. Some of the ugly scarring remained, though it would soon fade. My eye appeared normal, but I was still partially blind, and my hair was just starting to grow back in where it had been shaved for my multiple surgeries. Kelly had given me a lace front wig to wear but it itched so bad that I didn't have the patience to deal with it. Instead, I draped my longer hair over that side to conceal my butchered tresses,

The Coldest Love She's Ever Known

but it still looked a mess. I looked a mess. The last thing I wanted was a group of people around watching me.

My mama picked up on my uneasy expression and broke away from the crowd of family, friends and strangers around her. She wrung her hands before taking a deep breath and turned to everyone around her who was still looking at me with expectant stares in their eyes.

"Um... everyone help yourselves to some food. I'm going to get Sunday adjusted and then I'll be right back." With that said, she walked over to me and grabbed my hand. "You're probably tired. Is this all too much? I wasn't even thinkin'. I was just so happy to finally have you home and thought that a little bit of a celebration might—"

I put my hand up to stop her and shook my head. "It's okay, Mama, I understand. Thank you for doing all this for me. I'm just—I didn't want to leave Katie. I know I had to but... I just want to rest up so I can go back to the hospital to be with her."

Although I had been released from the hospital, my daughter Katera Kennedy, who I called 'Katie', was still in the NICU. There was an issue with her breathing that hadn't yet been corrected and she still hadn't been able to pass the auditory tests to show that she could hear.

In fact, Katie didn't respond to sound at all and it broke my heart to think that my baby would probably never be able to hear my voice. I thought about all the time that I'd spent talking to her while she was in my belly. It was a real possibility that she hadn't heard me any of those times.

Leaving the celebration behind me, I walked carefully with controlled steps, down the hall toward my room. My mama was walking behind me, giving me just enough space to not feel crowded though she was close enough to catch me if I fell. Even though I was recovering well, I was still adjusting to being partially blind in one eye and my motor skills were slightly impaired due to the trauma to my brain.

LEO SULLIVAN

When I stepped into my bedroom, I realized that some changes
had been made. A queen-sized bed had taken the place of the twin-
sized one that I'd left behind, new sheets were spread over the bed and
my teenage, girlish décor had been exchanged for something more
mature and appropriate for my age. Next to the bed was a crib and
it brought tears to my eyes. I couldn't wait until the moment when I
could place Katie inside.

"I tried to make sure that everything was comfortable for you
once you came back home," my mama said, speaking with her head
down as I looked around my room.

It was the same room that I'd lived in growing up until I moved in
with King. The moment that he brought up the suggestion that we live
together, I jumped at the opportunity and never again looked back.
Now I was back at square one. When so much progress should have
been made in my life, I was regressing instead.

"Do you like it?" she asked, and I realized that she had been waiting
on edge for me to respond. Turning to her, I gave her a genuine smile
and nodded.

"Yes, mama. I love it. And I want to thank you for doing this, I
only wish you didn't spend so much. How were you able to afford all
this stuff?"

The concern in my eyes only grew to another level when her gaze
leveled with the newly cleaned carpeted floor. She seemed afraid to
look at me.

"I—I… Well, that's something I need to speak to you about," she
began, clearing her throat. "Take a seat."

Pinching my lips together, I pulled them into my mouth and held
them in between my teeth as I did as she requested. Time seemed to
slow as I waited on edge while she closed the door and then turned
back to me. A long, protracted sigh escaped through her lips before
she finally lifted her head to speak to me.

"I—I have been keepin' something from you Sunday…"

My chest tightened and I felt like my breath was suddenly being constricted in my lungs. For some reason, I was expecting the worst.

"Your hospital stay was extremely expensive… You weren't on my policy once you went out on your own so I had to apply for you to receive Medicaid, but it wouldn't cover some of the treatments that the doctor said you would need in order to go back to living a normal life. The plastic surgery to fix the injuries to your face… getting your eye replaced… all of that stuff had to paid for. Not to mention the tests and treatments for the baby."

I swallowed hard and turned to look out the window, focusing on a blue bird that was perched on a limb outside. Part of me felt like I already knew what she was about to say.

"I received a visit from someone and… he told me that he would pay for whatever was needed. Then he came here last week and gave me the money to cover all of your and Katie's treatments and to get this room fixed up for your return home."

Shaking my head, I tried to force back my emotions but failed miserably. Before I knew it, I was swiping a tear from my cheek.

"If King gave you the money for this stuff, I don't want it. Caesar says that he's the reason I—"

"Sunday, that is a lie and you know it!" my mama interrupted, speaking through her teeth. "King did not order an attack on you. He would never do anything to hurt you or your child and you know that."

Defiance was all over my face, but I didn't say a word. I knew that she was right, and I also knew that my anger in the moment had nothing to do with what I was making it out to be. The fact was, King had escaped from prison, he was a wanted man, and some part of me felt like the dream I'd had of him visiting me in the hospital wasn't a dream after all. However, he hadn't been back since then and he hadn't contacted me once.

After seeing the reports of his escape on the news, I sent a message to his Instagram page asking for whoever was handling his account to have him contact me. Not once had I received a single response even though I'd messaged the page more than once. In this moment, I was definitely angry about something, but my anger had nothing to do with me feeling like King had asked someone to kill me. I was angry that he had met with my mama on multiple occasions but was keeping his distance from me.

"I don't care if that's true or not. Caesar believes that King did and he's my fiancé and Katie's father—"

"Does he know he's your fiancé and Katie's father?" my mama interrupted, folding her arms over her chest. She narrowed her eyes at me, making her disdain for Caesar obvious.

I countered by matching her posture. "What do you mean? Of course, he knows. He's been working! He's busy and that's the only reason he isn't here right now."

"Sunday—" she began and then stopped to drop the frustration from her tone. "Sunday, Caesar has not been to see you or Katie since he was released from the hospital over a month ago. He hasn't contributed a dime toward anything that I had to buy nor has he bothered to ask if anything was needed. You went through a whole facial reconstruction surgery and he didn't bother to show."

"He didn't know about it!" I defended, feeling fresh tears stinging my eyes. "I didn't have a chance to tell him about it."

It was true. Caesar and I hadn't spoken on the phone since he left. We'd only been communicating through texts because he said he was heavy in the streets, working to be able to get our lives back on track.

Truthfully, I was so hurt by how much he avoided looking at me when I was disfigured that I was purposely avoiding any conversation about my face.

"Rest up, baby girl," my mama suddenly said to me. I didn't have to look up to see her expression. I could hear the grief in her voice.

"Rest up and when you're ready, I'll drive you back up to the hospital to see Katie."

I nodded and forced myself to hold it together until she left out of the room and closed the door firmly behind her. The exact second it shut, the fragile levy holding in my emotions broke and I was overcome by the pressure of it all.

My daughter needed my strength and when I was back at her side, I would make sure to be strong. But, in this moment, I had to release.

Chapter Thirteen

King

"Yo, just say the word, King, and I could have this bitch ass nigga takin' a permanent dirt nap right along with his brother. I'm so close, I can see the whites in his eyes."

"Nah, stand down," I replied to Dolo, though I wanted nothing more than to give him the word to go ahead. "Just keep your eyes on him."

To be clear, I didn't give a fuck about Caesar's life, and before everything was said and done, I would make sure he received payment for his actions, but that time wouldn't be now. I didn't allow others to handle shit that was for me to deal with personally.

"I'm watching this nigga like he the plug, and my supply is on E. Ain't a corner in this building that he can walk to where I can't see him."

Chuckling at Dolo's way of putting things, I glanced out of my front windshield just as Sunday stepped off the bus. Clasping the edge of her jacket in her hands, she took a quick glance at her surroundings before pulling the yarn hat down low over her forehead, ducking her eyes and taking off in the direction of her mother's house. She was trying to blend in, but all she was did was make herself stand out.

No matter how hard she tried, Sunday could never blend in, not in my opinion. That's how it had been since the beginning because of how I felt about her. Now, she stood out because her fear of everything and everyone trailed her like a dark cloud. She was skittish, and it made her seem like an easy target for anyone looking to take advantage of a woman who appeared to have something worth protecting so desperately. She was only trying to protect her life, but street niggas would assume there was something more.

I had been trailing her every day for weeks since she came home from the hospital, making sure that she wasn't harmed whenever she went to visit her daughter. She always traveled to the hospital first thing in the morning and left in time to catch the bus that would get her home right before the sun set at night. While she was home, I always had someone stationed outside her residence to ensure her safety, someone I could trust.

The word was that the men who had almost killed her were still around, even though I hadn't been able to catch up with them yet. It was a given that one day they would come back to complete the job they'd started, so whether Sunday knew it or not, her life was in danger.

"He took the bait. They are on the move," Dolo said, referring to Caesar and the girl who we'd paid to capture his attention for the night. "She ain't even have to put in no real work to convince this nigga either. I should ask for half the money back."

"Yo' cheap ass would say something like that." I laughed, running my hand over my face. "As long as she gets the job done, she's earned it."

"True shit. I'll let you know when we get to the spot."

I ended the call and then paused when I realized I had an unanswered text message. There was no surprise that it was from

Makita. She'd been hitting my phone up regularly, either to give me updates about how things were with my team or to tell me how much she missed us being together. I appreciated her loyalty, but I was trying to keep my distance. No matter how she felt, there was no way I could give her what she wanted.

Blowing a burst of air through my mouth, I looked up and searched around for Sunday. The walk from the bus stop to her mom's crib was about eight blocks long, but it was a straight shot. Leaning up, I narrowed my eyes and peered down the sidewalk, wondering why I didn't see her anywhere around. I had only looked down for less than a few minutes. How could I have possibly lost her so fast?

"Where the fuck did she—"

Tap! Tap! Tap!

Flinching, I instinctually gripped the handle of my gun before turning to my left toward the source of the sound. When I saw the person standing there, my jaw almost dropped. I was looking at the last person I expected to see.

"Malik, I know you're in there!"

A smile teased the edge of my lips as I watched Sunday bending forward, trying her hardest to see through the dark, limousine tints on my ride. Her eyes were narrowed, her nose was wrinkled as if she smelled something rank, and her pouty lips were poked out in annoyance. Her angry face was one of the many things I loved about her.

"Stop yelling my government out like that. You work for the Feds or somethin' now?" I joked, rolling down the window.

It wasn't until I saw her angry expression fold into shame that I became aware of the ironic nature of my joke. Though I never believed she would have turned on me, many suspected that the reason I took on the murder charge in exchange for letting Sunday free was because

I thought she would talk and give the Feds information on not only me, but my whole operation.

I wasn't surprised that people thought it, though it wasn't true. Most niggas in my position would have let her go down for it all, being that she had a clean record and a better chance of escaping the charges, but that wasn't how I moved. I couldn't let her spend a day locked up for something that I knew she was only involved in because of me.

"I never told on you, and I never would have," she said, her voice almost so low that I didn't hear it.

I nodded. "I know."

A few quick moments of silence passed before Sunday seemed to suddenly remember what she had come over about.

"Why are you following me? Do you think I haven't seen you following me the past few days?" She cocked her head to one side and glared at me with her arms folded over her chest.

Past few weeks, actually, I corrected her in my mind but kept my mouth closed.

Dropping my eyes, I took her in, enjoying the beautiful sight that I was finally able to observe up close and personal after keeping my distance for so long. She teetered on the balls of her feet as I took my time before responding to her question. After all the time that we'd spent together, I still made her nervous.

"I'm just makin' sure you're safe. Is that a crime?"

Her brows rose. "Do you really want me to answer that?"

I had to laugh at that, though I fully understood what she meant. It wasn't wrong in the normal sense, but I was a wanted man with a price on my head, large enough to make somebody 'hood rich.' Simply taking a breath of fresh air that hadn't been given to me by the Feds was a crime.

"Nah, you ain't gotta answer that." A few moments passed before I nudged my head toward the empty passenger seat by my side. "Why don't you get in? Let me talk to you for a minute."

Sunday bit her bottom lip, and I watched as her eyes rose to the sky. Her mother told me that Sunday was partially blind in one eye and had some other impairments that she would have to adjust to over time. Looking at her then, I couldn't see anything but perfection.

"I don't know about that. I…" She let the last word hang in the air before clamping her mouth shut, appearing nervous for some reason I couldn't understand. When she opened her mouth again, she spoke, and I couldn't believe what she said.

"I heard the guys who did this to me say that you were the one who sent them. They said they were part of The JDBs."

My expression pinched. "That's bullshit. Whoever said that was lying. Trying to set me up."

She rolled her eyes and rested her weight on one hip. "Where have I heard that before? I guess everyone is trying to set you up, huh? Did somebody set you up for the murder of those two federal marshals that the news said you're responsible for?"

Sucking a sharp burst of air through my nose, I cut my eyes away from her before replying.

"There is a lot of shit I've done that I'm not proud of," I began and then turned back to meet her eyes. "But I've never been the type of nigga to lie about what I've done. You know that."

"Oh really? You mean like how you were supposed to be my man but was tonguing Makita down in the prison visitation room?" she shot back with fire.

I scrunched up my nose, trying to figure out what the hell she was talking about and how we got to this subject.

"Visitation room?" I paused, thinking for a moment. "If I was tonguing Makita down, that must've been right when I first got locked up. She was bringin' me dope and that's how she passed it to me—through her mouth. I had her do it because she didn't mean shit to me and I wouldn't give a fuck if she got caught. I needed money on the inside, but I would've never made you do no shit like that."

Defiant as ever, she crossed her arms in front of her chest and turned away from me, purposefully dodging my eyes. Her jaw flexed as she chewed the inside of her cheek. I knew that our past history was affecting her; she wanted to believe me, but it was easier to hate. Right now, she had a child with a man who had told her that I was the enemy and her life was less complicated if she took his side.

"Just stop following me," she said before doing a quick about face.

Before I could stop her, she took off in a jog across the street, rushing to increase the distance between us. For a moment, I thought about jumping out to follow her but then decided against it when I saw a patrol car turn onto the block. Although I'd been in hiding for a while, the police were constantly on the lookout for me. More than a few times I'd seen them stationed outside of Sunday's mom's crib, waiting to see if I'd come over.

Sighing, I ran a weary hand over my face and then grabbed my phone.

Bingo, I thought as I read the text from Dolo.

He had Caesar right where we wanted him, so it was time to move.

Chapter Fourteen

Sunday

"Yesss, Sunday, you did that!"

Holding up the sealed bag of freshly pumped breast milk, I grinned from ear-to-ear. Only new moms understood the sense of accomplishment that came from being able to pump more than a few ounces of milk at a time. It was even more enjoyable for me because I never thought that I would breastfeed since most women around me didn't. In my mind, it was the way that I took care of my baby.

At the moment, there wasn't much that I could do for Katie but feed her. She was still in the NICU, and I wasn't able to stay there with her. During the day, I tended to her, changed her diapers, cleaned and breastfed her, but when I went home, I felt like I was no longer her mother. Being able to do this one thing meant everything.

Just as I was attaching the breast pump to my other breast, the doorbell chimed. Groaning, I set the contraption down on the table next to the rocker that I was in and hurried to fix up my blouse.

"One minute!" I yelled, although I was positive that whoever was at the front door couldn't hear me.

I stood and was about to start toward the front of the house before pausing for a second to grab my pepper spray. I'd finally been able to convince my mama that I was comfortable enough to be home alone so she could go to work, but to be honest, I was tense until the moment that she came home. She worked nights as a nurse's assistant, and even though I knew she couldn't afford to miss any more checks over me, being alone at night was still hard.

With the spray in my hand, I crept toward the door on the tips of my toes, praying that when I looked outside, I'd be greeted by a friendly face. Leaning forward, I was about to press my face against the door to look through the peephole when whoever was on the other side began knocking with so much force, it was like they were trying to break down the door. I jumped so high that it was a wonder that I didn't hit the ceiling.

"Sunday, open up! It's raining hard as hell out here!"

"Caesar?" I frowned. It had been a while since I'd heard from him outside of a few texts and calls every now and then.

"Yeah, who else would it be? Open up!"

When I opened the door, I wasn't sure what to expect.

"What are you doing here?" I said with more aggression than I'd intended but less anger than I actually felt.

Although I hadn't mentioned it to anyone because I was tired of people pitying me for my circumstances, I was pissed at how Caesar had treated me and his daughter since leaving the hospital. He was basically acting as if we didn't matter. I understood that his life had changed drastically, just as mine had, but that was no reason for him to treat the ones who loved him so poorly.

"What you mean what am I doin' here? I came to see you and my daughter!"

With his nose curled into a snarl, he pushed by me into the house, scanning the living room with suspicion in his eyes.

"What other nigga you had in here got you actin' like that? It seems like you ain't want me in here."

"I don't!" I shouted, positioning my hands on my hips. "I haven't heard from you since you left the hospital except for random texts and short calls every now and then. You haven't gone to see your daughter *once* since the day we found out that she could be autistic, and you stopped coming to see me once you saw my face. I guess once you realized that we weren't perfect, you decided to bounce, huh?"

Caesar looked up at me with wide eyes, as if he were seeing me for the first time.

"Your face!" he said, gawking at me as I stood in the light. "How in the fuck did you get it fixed? You're beautiful again."

Walking forward, he grabbed me by my chin, pinching it between two of his fingers as he inspected me like I was under a microscope. I scowled as I snatched away. This was disgusting.

"I'm beautiful *again*?"

"Yeah," he replied, not at all catching my attitude. "This shit even looks better than before. They hooked your ass up. Did they fix your eye?" He waved his hand in front of the eye he was referring to. "I mean—can you see?"

My jaw nearly dropped. "If you're asking if I can see out of it again, the answer is no. So, you can stop with all the compliments and go back to how you were before when you didn't want me because I was ugly."

For the first time, Caesar seemed to realize what I was saying. Looking somewhat uneasy, he crossed his arms in front of his chest and shook his head.

"Nah, see, you takin' shit personal. Just because I said all that stuff 'bout your face didn't mean I didn't love you or think you were beautiful anymore," he said, backing away. He sat on the arm of the sofa behind him, and I watched as his face softened, giving me a glimpse of the man that he once was before everything went crazy between the two of us.

"It's just—seeing you like that hurt me. You don't have anything to do with this street shit, but you got pulled into it because of me. It broke my heart to see your face like that, and it breaks my heart to see my daughter struggling. I feel guilty; if it weren't for me, none of this would've happened."

"There is nothing wrong with Katie," I battled back at him, feeling tears build up in the corner of my eyes. "What she's going through was part of her life's story either way. But the difference between you and me is that, though she'll be different from a lot of people around her, I don't see anything she's gone through as a disability. She'll just have to work harder, and we will have to work harder as her parents to give her a good life. The life that she deserves."

Nodding, Caesar looked away from me, but I could still see the doubt in his eyes.

"Yeah, you're right," is what his mouth said, but his expression showed something different.

I realized the unconditional love I had for Katie was something that he simply didn't share for her... or for me.

"You can leave now," I told him and began to walk back to the door. "I need to finish pumping milk for our baby and get ready to see her in the morning."

"I want to go with you."

Standing, Caesar came over and reached out for me. I stood still as a statue as he gripped both of my arms and then ran his hands over my skin. He was looking at me with stars in his eyes, but I also noticed that he was marveling over my surgery, inspecting every inch of my face up close.

I wasn't convinced that this sudden change in him wasn't due to the fact that I was 'back to normal' in the physical sense. Through our time together, Caesar had often joked that I was a trophy wife, and it was no secret that he openly enjoyed the fact that people credited him for being the one to steal King's girl.

I saw the look in his eyes when men stole a glance at me; he enjoyed it. His pride and ego loved being able to call the girl everyone wanted his girl. That's how I knew, when I first saw my face after waking up from the coma, that he would leave me. It was a hard pill to swallow, but he was shallow.

"You don't need to go with me," I said, pushing him away. "I'm good to go on my own."

"I wasn't asking," he replied with grit in his tone. "You're my woman, and she's my daughter. I'm going with you, so hit ya moms up and let her know I'll be stayin' over tonight."

My eyes screwed tight. "Excuse me?"

"Is that a problem?" he asked, staring at me with accusing eyes. "I used to stay over here with you before we got our own place, so why I can't now? You got another nigga who been over here visitin' you?"

"What?" I frowned, playing off my anxiety.

In the back of my mind, I couldn't help but think about King and feel guilty. I knew that it showed all over my face, and I hoped that Caesar couldn't see it.

"No, I haven't had anyone seein' me over here. I'm not worried 'bout anything but my daughter."

"Just checking," he replied, but the suspicion and doubt were still in his eyes.

"Well, if you don't mind, I was pumpin' milk for Katie, and I need to finish."

The arm of the chair that Caesar was on creaked under his weight. He shifted his position and then shrugged.

"Go ahead. I just wanna talk to you, so as long as you're listenin' and your mouth still works, I'm good," he said.

I hesitated and gave him a hard look. There was definitely a lot of skepticism on my part about whether or not we were on good enough terms for me to be comfortable taking off my top in front of him, even if it was just to pump. Then, I took another moment to look at him— to *really* look at him—and I saw how hard he was trying to act normal though he wasn't. For someone who had always been so athletic and strong, he was winded, breathing hard like he'd run a few miles before walking to the door.

"How did you get here?" I asked, for the first time thinking about how he didn't have a car.

The car that he used to drive, the Benz that King bought for me, I'd given my mama to use for work. Until I got used to seeing out of only one eye, I refused to drive it.

"I caught a ride." He seemed agitated in his response. "Yo, can I get some water or somethin'? It's hot as hell in here."

"Yeah." I nodded, realizing that he'd broken into a sweat. "Go ahead and help yourself to whatever you want in the kitchen. I'm about to start pumping."

Hesitating for a moment, I watched as he took a deep breath before standing up from his seat and then slowly made his way to the kitchen. Although he was trying hard to control it, he was walking with a limp, and there was a lump poking out from the oversized sweatshirt that he was wearing.

Does he still have the... colostomy bag? I couldn't help but wonder. A wave of nausea came over me, and I swallowed hard to force it down.

With a heavy exhale, I shook the thought from my mind and began my walk down the hallway into my room to return to what I was doing before Caesar decided to stop by. It was strange seeing him after so much time had passed. In the back of my mind, I had imagined that life had gone back to normal for him while I'd been suffering through my new reality. Now, I saw that neither of us had managed to end up unaffected by what we'd been through.

Maybe that's why he's been so distant, I thought, feeling like I was understanding his struggle for the first time.

Caesar had always had a lot of pride. To be technically handicapped and to have to look at me and his daughter, who were also suffering from the things that had happened that night, probably pained him in the worst way. He was a man who couldn't protect his family when it mattered; the realization of all that surfaced every time he saw us, I was sure. That was possibly the reason why he stayed away.

"Do you remember anything else about that night other than what you told me?" Caesar asked, walking into my bedroom with a red cup in his hand. One look in his eyes told me that he was high. Most likely, he was still taking pain pills.

I didn't bother to look up as I attached the pump to my breast and then turned it on.

"No, I told you everything I remember."

"Nobody said any names except for that one you heard... Daze?"

"Yes, that was the only name."

To be honest, I really wasn't thinking all that hard because I didn't want to relive that moment.

"I need you to think long and hard about it and tell me what you can remember. It's important. I need to find the niggas who did this to me—to us," he corrected himself. "As soon as I can, I'ma handle them. You know what I mean?"

Though I nodded, I really didn't. How in the hell would he be able to do anything in the condition that he was in? It looked like it was a struggle for him to simply walk to the kitchen.

"Aye, you got any of those pills left? The percs they gave us both after the surgeries?"

Nodding my head, I pointed to my dresser across the room. "Over there. You can have them."

He was only too happy to oblige himself and I focused on my current task.

"Damn," he said, all of a sudden, and his tone made me raise my eyebrows.

When I looked up, he was staring hard at my chest. It was partially covered, but the small bits that he could see nearly had him salivating at the mouth.

"I know shit has been crazy ever since this stuff happened, but I was hoping that we could go back to how it used to be. I miss you."

Lifting my head, I gave him an even look but didn't say anything. In my mind, I had a lot of questions, but I also couldn't say that I didn't miss having him around, especially during times like this, when I was home all alone.

"We can work on it," I finally said. "I would love for you to be with us, me and Katie, but it's going to take time for me to trust that you'll never leave us again."

Caesar walked over, dragging his feet as he made his way to me. I looked in his face and tried to ignore the way that he was staring at me as if in awe of what he saw. It wasn't anything like how he'd looked at me when I first woke up from my coma before my face was changed.

"I won't leave. What man in his right mind could walk away from someone as beautiful as you?"

Bowing my head, I focused back on the task at hand, so when morning came, I could feed my baby. However, I couldn't rid the thought in my head that the only reason Caesar was dealing with me was because I'd gotten plastic surgery. King loved me no matter how I looked, but it was obvious that Caesar didn't.

Chapter Fifteen

King

"How far out are you?"

Glancing down at the navigation screen on my dash, I checked the ETA for my next destination.

"About five minutes," I replied.

"I can't wait to see you," Makita said in a melodious, flirty tone that she'd been using more and more in her conversations with me. "You've been away for so long, I kinda feel like you've been avoiding me."

"Never that, love," I said, though it was only partially true.

"Good. The door is unlocked, so you can just come inside. I've got a surprise for you."

I hadn't been exactly avoiding her, I'd been avoiding the conversation she would want to have once I saw her. At this point, I couldn't avoid meeting up with her any longer. Besides being my ex and the woman who had been by my side while I was serving time, Makita was my friend and a much-needed member of my crew. She was handling things that the streets taught me to only allow men to do, and she was completing the tasks better than they did.

As promised, I pulled into her driveway five minutes later, and I couldn't help but raise my brow at how she was living. Although she'd never been one to live in anything less than luxury, her current crib was on a different level. While I was locked up, I knew that I needed her, but from the looks of things, she needed me, too. In all the time before I pulled her into my fold and had her running my operations while I was locked up, she had never lived this good.

Makita's home was plush with wall to wall, expensive Persian carpeting and high cathedral ceilings, which elegant chandeliers hung from. Pricey paintings adorned the walls of the hall that I traveled through as I walked in, listening to the sound of talking over the blare of a television. When I stepped into the large living room, I was surprised to see Gunner sitting with Makita.

After catching up with Caesar the day before, there was nothing more that I wanted to do than to put a bullet in his head. It wasn't even about the fact that he was with Sunday now, but for the reason that he was mistreating her when she and their daughter needed him most. That was some shit that only lame niggas did. You didn't disrespect the people who held you down. That was one of the reasons that I was still dealing with Makita on any level.

By the time I arrived at the meet up spot, Bulletproof and Dolo had already roughed Caesar up enough to have him scared shitless. The moment he saw me step through the door of the abandoned condo unit, he immediately began to beg for his life.

"I'm not goin' to kill you," I had told him. "You have Sunday and Katera to thank for that."

His eyes screwed tight in confusion. "Sunday and who?"

Snorting a burst of air out through my nostrils, I shook my head in disbelief. This shit was pathetic. The nigga didn't even know his own daughter's name.

"What have you found out 'bout the men who killed your brother and raped Sunday?" I asked him, deciding to move on to the principle matter at hand. "You've been lookin' for them, right? What have you found?"

His pupils scrolled from me to the ceiling before his jaw dropped slightly, as if he were dumbfounded.

"Um..."

My eyes narrowed. "You ain't found out shit? Somebody killed your brother, tried to kill you, your girl, and your child, but you ain't found out shit since you been beatin' the streets all this time?"

"I—"

"You have been lookin' for them, right? Ain't that what you been tellin' Sunday? Or are you still trying to convince her that the hit was ordered by me?"

Caesar tensed, clenching his jaw tight. "They said your name."

"Yeah, but you know better than that shit," Dolo said, tapping Caesar in the back of his head with the barrel of his gun. "That shit was sloppy. Plus, The JDBs don't kill babies and rape women. Stop tryin' to play stupid, nigga."

Not responding, I watched Caesar's expression change, showing that he knew what Dolo said was right. We all knew it was true; the only reason he'd held on to that fake ass story about me being behind the hit was so that Sunday, and whoever else he could convince, would hate me for it.

"The only thing I know is that my girl said a nigga by the name of Daze had raped her. She also saw the face of the man who shot her... a white boy. I don't really remember him, but he was part of Daze's crew."

Locking eyes with Dolo, a few unspoken words passed between us. Daze was a small-time hustler who could've made it to big time in any other city but mine. I didn't fuck with him on any level, and I put word out that my crew better not either. He wanted to be a JDB in the worst way, but my conscience wouldn't allow it. He was known to be a merciless killer; had no problem killing innocent women and children if it got him what he wanted. I couldn't be down with anyone like that.

"What else you found out? You know where they are?"

Caesar shook his head. "Nah."

"This nigga ain't good for shit!" Dolo scowled at him while stroking his gun with his finger.

I knew he felt the same way that I did. Thinking Caesar might actually be useful was a waste of time, and so was he; a better option would be to put a bullet in his skull and keep it moving. The only thing stopping me was Sunday. I wasn't lying when I said she her and her daughter were the only reasons that I was keeping him alive. If I killed him, she would never forgive me.

"Yeah, but he's goin' to change that," I said with my eyes still on Caesar's face. "From now on, you work for me. In two days, I'll be back. If you don't have any information that's of use to me, shit ain't gon' be sweet. I suggest you get to work beatin' the streets and try to find somethin' good."

When I met back up with him two days later, he had something for me, and the shit made me sick to my stomach. Gunner, one of the niggas I trusted with not only my life but my mama's life, had betrayed me. From what Caesar said, while I was locked up, Gunner had been trying to rally a team of men to find the dope and money I'd hidden after leaving Colombia. He wanted to get his hands on it, so he could make his own team and take over The JDB under his rule. Once I escaped, his plan changed but only slightly.

Now he was planning to get me to tell him where my stash was, pretending to help me flip it since I couldn't do it myself, and then he would call the Feds to turn me in and collect the bounty on my head. I didn't want to believe it, but only my closest partners even knew that I had stashed that dope and money. I hadn't told anyone outside of Makita and Gunner; everyone else thought that I'd given it all to Bulletproof and Dolo before I surrendered in exchange for Sunday.

"Man, it's good to see you, nigga!" he said, standing up to greet me.

I slapped hands with him before pulling him in for a hug, looking curiously over his shoulder at Makita who was sitting behind. She had managed to lure Gunner there, but it didn't seem that he suspected a thing.

Not saying anything to me, she allowed the desire in her eyes to do all the talking. Standing to her feet, she sashayed across the carpet, gave me a hug, and kissed me sweetly on my cheek. She didn't let go and held onto my hand once the embrace was over. The smell of her perfume should have gotten to me, but my mind was elsewhere, suspended in a myriad of intricate thoughts.

"Yeah," I replied to Gunner. "It's been a while. I haven't seen you since y'all broke me out at the courthouse. What you been up to?"

Shrugging, he shook his head. "Not too much. Just had to lay low for a minute. My girlfriend found out about my side bitch, and she's been threatening to tell the police that I helped get you out of prison. I've just been keepin' my distance. Didn't want her crazy ass startin' shit."

"And that's the only reason you been layin' low?" Makita asked. She pulled her hand from mine and crossed her arms in front of her chest as she gave him a sideways look.

With a slight frown, Gunner shrugged. "Yeah. Shit, I thought we was all kinda layin' low for a while. The Feds know that The JDB broke you out. I'm surprised you still here to be real 'bout it. You got to leave the country. There is a massive manhunt like I never seen before. How you been gettin' around?"

I felt Makita's heated stare on me, and I knew what she was thinking. She'd been telling me the same thing about leaving. On more than one occasion, she'd said that we needed to charter a plane to take us to Cuba, but there was just one problem; she wasn't the woman I wanted to go with me.

"I still got a few tricks up my sleeves," I vaguely replied. "You know they got a price on my head. I'm an enemy of the government, and they dropping a few mill for my life. You heard 'bout that?"

Gunner's brows shot up to the sky. "Word? Damn, I ain't know that. That's a lot of bread."

"Enough to make friends turn to enemies," Makita said and took a step forward.

Her eyes were filled with fury as she glared at him. Gunner caught the change in her disposition, and he frowned as he looked back and forth between the two of us, reading her expression. Just a few moments ago, they'd been sitting together, talking like friends, and now she'd swapped the script.

"Nah, it ain't that much." His face went stone cold as he stared back at her. "Ain't no amount of money in the world worth turning on someone you consider your brother."

I nodded in agreement with what he was saying, although I doubted that he truly believed it.

"You called Shotti?" I asked Makita, attempting to break the tension. "We need all hands on deck to get everything and bring it back."

With a nod, Makita pulled her attention away from Gunner and checked the watch on her wrist.

"I called him but let me grab my phone so I can see how far out he is."

With one last hard look at Gunner, she turned on her heels and sashayed away, liberally swaying her hips.

"Yo, King, what's up with yo' girl?" Gunner's nose curled up "Why she lookin' at me like that?" He took a step closer to me to make sure that he wasn't overheard. "She got a nigga feelin' like I need to be explainin' some shit that I don't even know 'bout."

"I think everyone is on edge right now," I told him with an even tone. "When you bring money into the game, shit begins to change."

He wagged his head in a sharp nod. "You right 'bout that. Matter of fact, while you was locked out, there was some shit goin' on that I didn't like to see. I ain't gon' mention it now since we got business to take care of, but I'll say this…" He took a step even closer. "Even though she held it down while you was locked up, make sure you keep your eyes on ole girl. And, to be honest, I don't think we need Shotti. Me and you could get this dope on our own. The less people around, the less muthafuckas we have to trust. Especially that one."

Just in case I wasn't aware that he was referring to Makita, he cut his head back in the direction that she'd walked when she left and then widened his eyes as he took a few paces back. Just as he'd returned to where he'd been standing before, she came back into the room with her cell phone in hand.

"Shotti should be here any moment. I told him to bring a few duffle bags with him, so he had to stop to pick some up."

The sound of that seemed to break Gunner out of his serious state, and one edge of his lips hinted at a smile.

"Damn, you hid that much shit? We gon' need duffle bags for all of it?" he asked.

He was elated. Dressed in a gray Nike jogging suit with black Yeezy sneakers, and his banger stashed in his waistband, he rubbed his hands together, mentally already calculating how much money was about to be made.

Chapter Sixteen

King

With a solemn expression on his face, Shotti drove without doing much speaking while Gunner sat in the passenger seat, speaking more than usual. He was almost giddy as he bounced from subject to subject, his excitement about what he thought was our current mission showing all over his face.

I sat in the back, watching everything around me as I mediated on my thoughts. It was in the moments when you were down that you found out who your true friends were. Gunner had been with me during many times when it seemed that we were experiencing our lowest moments, but he'd stuck with me, mainly because he didn't have any other choice. However, the one time that I was locked up, and he knew that there was money on the table, the true side of him came to the surface. It was hard for me to believe that my own partner since I was a kid would try to rob me.

"Shit been crazy since you been gone, King, but I'm happy that you home. It's just fucked up because of the circumstances, but I did take money by your mama's house and made sure our business accounts was straight with the money going to Makita, as you instructed."

"Yeah, I heard," I casually said, remembering the look on Gunner's face when I told him to have Makita handle my money instead of him. He didn't like bringing her in, but she had a degree in accounting and finance. To me, it made sense.

"I don't know what she did with that shit once I handed it over to her, but I did what you said," he added with a hint of disdain in his voice.

"You know why I couldn't let you handle that much money, Gunner. Makita has a degree for that shit, but that wasn't the only reason."

A sheepish expression crossed his face. I could see it through the rearview mirror. A while back, Gunner had a bad addiction to snorting coke and messed up some money while he was dealing with it. The only thing that kept him alive back then was the fact that I considered him a close friend. However, since then, I'd stripped him of dealing with any large amount of money on any level.

"Man, I know where you going with this, and yes, I did fuck up. But as you know, when you got locked up, I had millions stashed too. I still got stacks saved, maybe not as much as you, but I have some. Yeah, when you first went away, I relapsed for a little while, but I came back from that. Since you've been gone, I followed your lead, bought real estate, invested in stocks, and opened a few businesses—cleaning services run by some hard-working Mexican chicks. I got my own fuckin' money, King. You know that."

"Yeah, I hear you," was all I said as we turned off highway 1-85 onto Georgia 400.

Suddenly, Gunner turned to Shotti and said facetiously, "Damn, nigga, you look like you headed to a funeral instead of to pick up a thousand kilos of coke. Why you look so serious and shit?"

Caught off guard by his question, Shotti chuckled. "Nah, nigga, I'm excited, but it's just so much shit going on."

"Yeah, I feel you," Gunner said, staring intensely at him. Then he turned and looked out the window at the landscape around us.

"Man, where the fuck y'all taking me?" Gunner asked. His hand moved to his side like he was removing his banger from his waist.

Shotti cut his neck toward him, also catching the move.

"Chill, nigga!" His tone was elevated. "Why you pulling out your strap?"

"'Cause I don't like the vibe in here. You all quiet and shit, plus you driving all the way to Cummings. Ain't no niggas livin' out here."

Despite the seriousness of the situation, I snorted air out of my nostrils in somewhat of a suppressed chuckle. He was right about that.

"That's right," I told him. "That's what makes this the perfect spot to stash some shit."

It made sense, but Gunner wasn't feeling it. His sixth sense had picked up on a different vibe, and he wasn't letting it go.

"Turn around! Take me back!"

"Don't aim that fuckin' pistol at me!" Shotti yelled, taking his eyes off the road.

The car slightly swerved just as we passed a state trooper in the next lane. Shotti was only slightly speeding, doing about seventy miles an hour in a sixty-five. We didn't see the state trooper at first because it was on the other side of an eighteen-wheeler, but I saw him the second that he slid into our lane and started to drive behind us.

"Fuck!" Shotti cursed under his breath.

"Just drive the speed limit," I said, fighting the urge to turn around and look out the back window. If the cop saw it, that would have been a sure sign to pull us over.

"Man, we don't need to get pulled," Gunner said, slapping the barrel of the gun into the palm of his other hand.

"Put up that gotdamn gun, nigga," Shotti demanded through clenched teeth.

"I am."

"Man, not under the seat! The fuck wrong with you?" Shotti screeched.

Frowning, Gunner lifted his hands and shrugged. "What you mean? This shit is hot; it has a body on it. I can't keep it on *me*."

"You sho-n-da-fuck ain't finna stash that shit in my whip and get me a case if we get pulled. Nigga, put that shit in your draws and get out and RUN if shit pop off!"

"Y'all, chill," I calmly said, but inside, I was worried as fuck.

I knew if we got pulled, it would be a wrap for me. The end of the road, possibly, if things didn't end well. They were talking about a hot gun, but there was a real possibility that as soon as this cop saw my face, I'd be gifted with a bullet between the eyes.

Chirp! Chirp!

My heart sank to my feet. Instinctively, my hand went to the gun that I had stashed on me. I took it out and tucked it under my leg as my heart raced in my chest.

"Fuck! What we gon' do now?" Shotti asked, looking at me for help.

"You got your license on you?"

"Yeah," he responded and stared out the rearview mirror.

I noticed him fumbling with something and glanced in his direction. It was the pistol I gave him before we left Makita's. For a moment, as I saw the jittery state that he was in, I regretted giving it to him. Shotti looked like he was about to lose his mind. Then again, he had good reason for it.

Georgia State Troopers were notoriously racist and aggressive rednecks with an attitude. Knowing that, my first instinct was to just shoot him in the face as soon as he stuck his head in the window, but my better judgement told me not to. I would just have to play it by ear.

The cop walked up; he had a potbelly with a huge, five gallon hat on his head. He wore a shit-colored uniform with mirror shades. His face was snow white, but his cheeks were rosy red. There was a wad of tobacco in his mouth that he chewed obnoxiously with his mouth wide open.

Sitting up straight in his seat, Shotti let the window down halfway. "Can I help you, Officer?"

"Yep," he replied with a country boy twang. "Let that window down some more, so I can see who's inside."

"Yes, sir."

Shotti complied and rolled down the window.

"Let me see your license and registration," the cop said and held onto his hat as a large truck passed along with other vehicles.

"Yes, sir."

The cop looked at Shotti's license and registration then stuck his head back in the window, scrolling his eyes first to Gunner and then to me.

"I'ma need to see some ID from you boys. Y'all live around here?"

I didn't answer; I was prepared to shoot when and if the moment came to that.

Gunner started to talk with the cop as he passed him his ID.

"I'll need yours, too."

"I left my wallet," I explained. "But my name is Tony Blackman."

The trooper gave me a hard look, as if he didn't quite believe my story, but then shrugged before walking back to his patrol car to run a check on our names.

It felt like he was gone forever before he finally returned. He passed the IDs over to Shotti.

"I'm not going to give you a ticket for speeding, and since all you boys' IDs and names check out, I'ma let you go this time. Have a nice day," he said and tipped his hat.

Frozen with shock and relief, none of us moved until the trooper was back in his car and had pulled off, driving back into traffic. As he drove off, I couldn't help but feel depleted, even fatigued. Since making it out of prison, I had experienced more drama than most people experienced in several lifetimes, and things were just getting started.

***

"This is the area right here," I said as we pulled into Lake Ellijay.

It was a dense forest of jungle, water, and wildlife for miles and miles as far as the eye could see, with so much foliage and masses of land it wasn't uncommon for people to get lost for days in the vastness.

"Man, this don't look right!" Gunner exclaimed as soon as we got out of the car.

"It's not supposed to."

"Ain't we gon' need some shovels or something to dig with?" Gunner asked as he walked through the thick bush of the forest, looking around suspiciously.

I quickly gave Shotti the signal to shoot him as soon as we neared a big tree. Overhead, a flock of geese flew, making all types of noise just as Shotti pulled out his pistol and hesitated. That was all it took for Gunner to pounce on him with surprising quickness.

Blocka!

One lone shot rang out, causing more birds to take flight for the skies. At first, I didn't even know who was shot or where until I heard Gunner groaning in agony.

"Ohhh, shit, this nigga shot me!" he shouted as they tussled and fell to the ground.

Gunner had been shot in the neck. Blood gushed all over the forest floor, but he managed to scramble on top of Shotti and punched him several good times.

"Help me, King. This nigga crazy. He shot me!" Gunner yelled.

By then, he was whooping Shotti's ass with overhand rights, uppercuts, and knees to his nuts. Gunner had managed to pull Shotti's shirt over his head and began to beat his ass even more. Then h e wrestled the gun from his hand and stood. I couldn't help but reflect on what my mama used to say.

"A scared man will kill you."

Gunner was living proof of that; he was scared, and he was fighting for his life while bloody as a tampon.

He stood on wobbly legs as blood poured from his neck like an open fire hydrant in the summertime.

"Man, what da fuck is goin' on?" He staggered.

"You, Gunner. You set me up, got me sent to prison in the first place. You had me framed and plotted on the dope that I got stashed from the Colombians. That is what got you trapped right now. Greed."

As I talked, Shotti sat up. He was still punch drunk and leaking from both his mouth and nose.

"Nigga, is you crazy? You like a fuckin' brotha to me. We slept in the some fuckin' pissy bed, was hungry, and used to steal out of stores just to eat! Yeah, I fucked up, but I took care of your mama while you was gone and made sure Nikki was straight too. Now you tryin' to say I betrayed you for money? I made millions right along with you, and you know it," Gunner said with a stricken face as tears fell from his eyes.

~ 163 ~

His voice was guttural and strained as I looked down at him. He was on the brink of death as blood continued to pour from the gunshot wound in his neck. Pathetically, he began to sob even harder.

"You gotta get me to a hospital or I'ma die… Man, I'ma bleed to death if you don't help me. Please."

The entire right side of his sweat-suit was wet as he began to rock back and forth, like he was fighting the torment of dying and demise as he held the gun in his hand.

I took out my pistol and held it at my side. I can't even lie; I felt a pang of hurt in my heart. Gunner was like a brother to me, but I had to do what needed to be done.

"I'ma have to lie you down right here and send you into the next life. This life ain't meant for both of us. This is the end of the road for you—for us. Don't make this difficult," I said and then aimed the gun at his forehead.

In a flash, Gunner came up with his weapon and closed his eyes before squeezing the trigger several times…

Click! Click! Click! Click! Click!

"It's empty," I said, solemnly.

Stepping back, I watched him stagger as he looked at me with blood gushing from his neck. Then he looked at the gun in his hand and frowned. His free hand moved to his neck, an attempt to stop the bleeding. The bleeding seemed to worsen as blood spewed through his fingers.

Suddenly, he fell to his knees and I walked over, placing the gun to his forehead.

"Man, you making a big mistake. I would never betray you! Please, don't kill me. Help me, I need to go to the hospital. You gon' regret this one day if Shotti and that lyin' bitch told you that I betrayed you."

"Okay, I'll help you," I said, finally.

He looked up at me and his expression hinted at relief. Without hesitation, I shot him in the head, point blank. One shot blew his brains out on the forest floor.

He keeled over landing on his back with one of his legs awkwardly twisted underneath his body. I stood there in a daze; it felt like I had lost a piece of my soul. Gunner's eyes were stretched wide, staring at his next destiny.

"Man, you did what you had to do," Shotti said, using his shirt to wipe the blood from his face. "That nigga probably was always plotting on you. Fuck him! He lucky my finger's fucked up or I would have beat his skinny ass."

I wasn't buying it. Shotti was a coward and the more time that passed, the more I realized it.

"Shut up! Let's bury his body under these leaves and go!"

Chapter Seventeen

Sunday

"Who is supposed to pick you up?"

I looked up into the gentle and kind face of Ms. Beatrice, the nurse that I'd come to regard as family in such a short amount of time. She'd been instrumental in making sure that I was comfortable every time I came to visit Katie and even bent the rules a couple times to ensure that I could be with my daughter as much as possible.

"My fian—" I stopped short of calling Caesar my fiancé and sucked in a sharp breath. "I mean, her dad."

Ms. Beatrice's lips pursed into a straight line before she nodded her head.

"Well, there is no rush, as you know. I was able to get you into a vacant room where you and Katie can stay until he arrives. We don't have any additional mothers expected to come in to deliver today. However, as you know, things can happen unexpectedly, so I'll let you know if we end up needing the room."

Nodding, I hugged Katie to my chest and kissed the top of her forehead. I heard what she was saying, and I saw the worry lines in her forehead, but I was determined not to allow anything to steal my joy.

Today was a *huge* day.

After being in the hospital for so long, Katie was finally able to come home. She was still so small, but there was really no reason to keep her. She'd made a miraculous recovery after her near-tragic entrance into the world. Although she still hadn't passed any of the hearing screens, and I knew that I would have to work with a specialist to address the concerns around that, she was perfectly healthy otherwise and breathing on her own.

The hospital had a rule that once a newborn was released from the hospital, a member of the staff had to check the car seat before they were able to leave with the baby. For that reason, I'd asked Caesar to pick us up and he'd agreed to borrow his friend's car so that he could. He also told me that he would buy the car seat and install it prior to arriving, which brought me a little bit of joy that he was finally seeming to involve himself when it came to our daughter. However, it was now three hours after the time when he was supposed to be there, and he still hadn't arrived.

"Caesar, it's me, again," I said with tears in my eyes as I left yet another message on his voicemail. "Katie and I are still waiting for you. They have us in a room, but if you don't come before they need it back, they'll put her back in the NICU and I might not be able to take her home. Please, call me."

Hanging up the line, the thought of calling King came to mind but I quickly brushed it away. He was a wanted man and, after the police received a tip that he was still in the city, they'd been scouring the area like crazy. I no longer picked up on him watching me walk back and forth from the bus stop each day to visit Katie so I was sure that he knew they were on to him; might even have thought that I was the one who called them since the tip came in after the day that I caught him watching.

Another option was to call my mama, but I didn't want to go that route. She didn't know it, but I'd seen a write-up in her purse when she got home one night, saying that if she missed any more days of work, she would be at risk of losing her job. I couldn't ask her to take that gamble for me.

"Is there no one else you can call?" Ms. Beatrice asked me again about a half hour later.

Dropping my eyes to the floor, I shook my head. Katie was lying in my arms, sleeping snuggly against my breasts. She was like an angel, but I couldn't even bring myself to look at her right then. I was her mother and, yet again, I was helpless when she needed me.

"I called someone for you," Ms. Beatrice suddenly said in a small voice.

Snapping my head up, I frowned slightly as I looked at her. "Who?"

"There was a man ... he didn't leave his name, but he gave me a number and made me promise to call it if you ever needed him. He told me that I should consider calling him a *last resort*. I—I think that we are there now—at the point where he should be called. So, I did."

King, I thought, swallowing hard. She'd called a man and there wasn't a doubt in my mind that he was the one she'd dialed.

"I hope I didn't overstep," she said, sliding into a chair across from me.

Placing her hand on my arm, she silently beckoned me to look into her eyes. I did that, focusing in on her dark brown eyes which were shining with tears.

"I can tell that he's a man with many secrets and that he has probably done a lot of things in his life that he wouldn't want anyone to know. But..." She paused to lick dry lips. "I also know that when I looked into his face, I saw the deepest, truest, love and compassion there. He loved you and I know that he would never hurt you. Right now, you need someone you can depend on."

I nodded my head and swiped away a tear from my eye. She was right.

***

Less than thirty minutes later, I was sitting inside of the hospital lobby, staring out the glass doors when I saw an Audi with dark tints pull up, curbside. At the same exact moment, a few more cars drove up as well, all with dark tints, surrounding the black Audi.

"I think this may be your ride," Ms. Beatrice spoke up, watching the outside along with me.

"I think you're right."

Though the caravan of cars was discreet, I knew who was inside. King had arrived to pick me up, as promised by the simple 'okay' that he'd sent Beatrice's phone when he replied, but he made sure to have his soldiers on point to protect him. Even still, it was an incredible risk that he was taking by being there.

"Let me help you and Katie out."

Before I could object, she stood up, positioned herself behind me and grabbed the handles of the wheelchair that I was seated in.

"I can walk! I told you that I don't need this thing," I complained to her.

"It's hospital policy. Just relax and let me do my job," Ms. Beatrice replied. I didn't have to look up at her to know that she was sporting a smug smile.

The automatic glass doors opened, and I watched the Audi carefully as we neared it. Katie was wrapped up like a burrito in my arms, but I looked down at her when the bright sun hit her face and smiled when I saw her squinting her eyes. It was her first encounter with natural sunlight. Pulling the soft pink cap down further over her face, I adjusted her position toward me and hugged her tight.

"Thanks, Ms. B., I got it from here," I heard a voice say.

Looking up, my jaw nearly dropped when I saw King exiting from the back door of the Audi. He had a stern look on his face and his eyes were scanning his surroundings attentively. Wearing a black jacket with the hood pulled over his head, he pulled his hands out of the pocket of his black sweatpants and walked over to me.

"It's good to see you again, Malik. I hope you've been staying out of trouble."

At that, even King had to laugh. "Yeah, as much as I can."

When he lowered his head and brought his eyes to my face, I couldn't help but blush under his gaze. The love that Ms. Beatrice had mentioned seeing in his eyes? I saw it, too. To be honest, it had never left, but I had been too stubborn to notice. Now it was becoming clear to me that, outside of my mama, King was the only one I had. Even Kelly and I didn't talk as much anymore.

King already had a car seat for Katie secured in his car, and after I checked it thoroughly, I secured Katie inside. Before slipping into the backseat with her, I gave Ms. Beatrice a tight hug to thank her for everything she'd done for me and then tried to hold back tears as the vehicle began to drive away.

The car was completely silent the entire way to my mama's house as one of King's friends, who I didn't recognize, drove and he sat in the passenger seat. I marveled at the sight of my daughter during the ride, ignoring everything else around me. The amount of joy that I felt in my heart about finally being able to have her with me at every moment outweighed my anger at Caesar for letting us down, once again, and my fear for riding around in a car with a wanted criminal.

"I'm going to walk you to the door. I'll take out the car seat for you," King said when we arrived at our destination.

In a near panic, I jerked up in my seat and shook my head.

"No, you don't have to do that. If anyone sees you—"

"I'm good," King replied, interrupting me with a sharp tone. "You're a mother, bringing your newborn baby home. Ain't no fuckin' way I'm goin' to sit here and let you carry all this shit yourself. Once you get her out of the seat, you go ahead inside and I'll get everything else for you."

I jerked my head to the guy in the passenger seat. "Why can't he do it?" I asked. "Nobody is lookin' for him."

"How you know that?" the guy joked. He grinned wide, showing off a mouth full of gold teeth. "I'm guilty of a lot of things. Somebody always lookin' for me."

"Cut that shit out, Dolo," King said before turning his sharp gaze back to me. "Go."

At that moment, I knew there was no point in arguing further. Once King took that tone, he wasn't trying to negotiate. With a heavy exhale, I began to take Katie out of her car seat after scanning the area to make sure that it was free of police. There was no need for me to be so cautious; King was always aware of everything around him at all times. Still, after being away from him so long, I couldn't help it. Caesar was never as careful as King had always been when it came to matters of security... that much was obvious.

Once I was inside, I started to get Katie settled in her room. She was still sleeping, and I was eager to finally have her in her bassinet. So many nights had been spent with me staring at it, dreaming about the moment when she'd finally be in it. That time was now.

"Everything is inside. Where would you like me to put this?"

Hearing King's voice behind me, I turned around and tried to ignore the way that he lazily brought his eyes up from my backside to level his gaze at my face.

"Um... What is that?" I pointed to the large box that he was holding in his hands. It was gift-wrapped with a big bow on top.

"Something I got for the little princess," he said, placing the box down next to his feet.

Then he pulled out another box from his pocket that matched the larger one with a small bow on top.

"And this one is for you. Congratulations, Sunday. I'm proud of you."

Without waiting for me to respond, he placed the box on top of the larger one and then turned around to leave. I wanted to stop him; I felt like there was something that I needed to say, but my feet were cemented into the floor. I was paralyzed by the battle between my brain and my heart.

It was stupid to be with King; it had always been that way from the beginning. Being with him was dangerous. It brought enemies and danger to me that I hadn't earned on my own, the kind that came just because I was the street king's girl. I'd almost been framed for a triple homicide that I didn't commit, and I'd almost been killed in some street shit that probably involved him. Now, I had a child to think of, a baby who needed her mother alive. Being with him wasn't safe for me and it definitely wasn't safe for my child.

But as much as I knew it in my head, my heart was resistant to admit that it was true. My heart told me that being with King was the only place that I wanted, and needed, to be.

Chapter Eighteen

King

It was hard to leave Sunday, but I had too much business to tend to, so I couldn't stay. Someone had reported to the Feds that I'd been spotted and the manhunt for me was, once again, at an all-time high. Makita wanted me to believe that Sunday was the one who had alerted the police, but I knew that wasn't true. Somehow, she found out that I'd seen Sunday that day. I didn't doubt that she had eyes in the hood but what I did wonder is if her eyes were watching my movements or Sunday's. These days, she seemed more than a little too preoccupied with my ex.

With the Feds on hot pursuit, ready to bust a shot, the second they saw my ass, Makita had given me a key to her place so that I could use it to take refuge if it ever got to that point. I suspected that she really wanted me to stay with her until I made my next move, but I refused. She was a woman who had shown me some loyalty, but she was *still* a woman. One who claimed she loved me and was consistently trying to urge me to make things official because she knew I loved someone else. I couldn't trust her with my life.

When I stepped into Makita's house, I thought it was empty until I heard her voice echoing from the living room. She didn't know I was coming; I couldn't call her because along with the gifts that I'd left Sunday, I also left the burner phone that Ms. B. had called me on. I couldn't risk having it on me after she used it. If anything went wrong, or if someone happened to become suspicious by my arrival at the hospital, they could put pressure on her, and she would cave. Not only that, but I also wanted a way to stay in contact with Sunday.

"What do you *mean* he was there to see her? Where the fuck were you?"

Makita was furiously shouting to someone who must've been on the phone because she paused to listen to the response before speaking again.

"Look, I handled it the last time you were slipping on your job. You need to remember our agreement because, lately, you ain't been holdin' up your end of the plan. Don't think I didn't catch that shit you pulled with Gunner!"

Stopping mid-step, I frowned at the mention of Gunner's name. Suddenly, I no longer thought that she was speaking to one of her friends that she had posted up in the hood to watch me or Sunday. This was someone else.

"No, you called him out because you were tryin' to be slick and send a message to me, but I ain't havin' that. I got too much invested in this shit. Do what you're supposed to do and don't fuck up again."

By the time she hung up the phone, I was standing right behind her. When she turned around, she jumped almost three feet into the air and then began to laugh with relief.

"King, you scared the shit out of me!" she said with her hand pressed against her chest.

I wasn't amused and I wasn't feeling too patient either. I had questions that she needed to answer, or shit was going to get ugly, fast.

"Who was that on the phone?" I asked with a straight face.

Though I had my own suspicions, I wanted to watch her reaction. Makita was slick as grease and sly as a fox, but I'd taught her everything she knew about that. Having a father in the streets taught her the game but being with me was what groomed her into a boss. If she lied, I would know immediately.

"That was Caesar," she answered without hesitation and without any readable emotions on her face.

"Why did he call you? Y'all know each other?"

"In passing," she answered with a slight shrug. Turning, she walked away as she continued to explain.

"When you got locked up, he came to me, asking if he could be part of The JDB. He said that he needed the money because the low-level hustling wasn't gettin' him anywhere. I told him 'no', of course, but every now and then there was some menial task that I'd toss his way. Something I didn't want my hands involved in. I figured you wouldn't mind since whatever money he earned would also go to Sunday."

I didn't miss the dry hatred in her tone when she said her name. Her back was to me, but I could almost see her rolling her eyes. My senses were on high alert.

"So why he callin' you now? What agreement y'all got?"

She turned sharply in my direction, frowning. "We don't have any business together. The plan that I mentioned on the phone was the one you came up with. You told him that he works for you and as long as he brings you back news, he can stay alive. I simply reminded him of that."

I nodded. Her story sounded good, but it didn't feel right. "And what 'bout all that shit concerning Gunner? What that got to do with you?"

Her expression faltered, giving away to a hint of shame. "Gunner and I... uh, ..." She swallowed hard and began wringing her hands together. "We had a little fling when you went away. I was distraught and just desperate enough to do something with him." She rolled her eyes. "Caesar tried to hold it over my head after he told you about Gunner. He said that you would doubt my loyalty and was trying to push me into giving his desperate ass some money. I guess he's tryin' to get enough money up to ask Sunday to marry him. You know they are back together, right?"

No, I *didn't* know that Sunday was back entertaining that clown outside of him being the father of her kid, but I didn't respond.

"That nigga ain't gon' be around to do shit if he don't come at me with somethin' I can use. Matter of fact, I might go see 'bout his ass today. From where I'm standin' he's being a fucked-up father as it is and he's no use to me, so I need to cancel his ass. He ain't worth keepin' around."

"Wait!"

Makita shouted just as I was turning around to leave. I'd come over to speak business with her, to let her know that I'd decided for sure that I had to leave the country and needed to get things straight with my team before I went away, but that wasn't the pressing issue on my mind right then.

"What?" I asked with agitation as I turned around.

"He *did* tell me somethin' for you to use. I forgot to mention it when you started asking me all those questions." She let out a few dry chuckles. Nervous chuckles, if I'd ever heard any before.

"What he say?"

"He told me that... he said that he remembered one of the men who was with Daze that night. A white boy who goes by the name Ghost. Caesar saw them turning up at this club with this nigga named

Shawn who used to run dope out of Augusta a while back. He said they were there with a whole group, but he definitely recognized Daze and Ghost. The others may have been involved, but he wasn't sure."

I couldn't believe the shit I was hearing. "You tellin' me he *saw* the same niggas who killed his brother, raped and shot his girl and almost killed him and his kid, but he let them get away?"

Pushing her lips into a straight line, Makita nodded her head, but avoided looking me in the eyes. There was more to it than what she was saying, but I didn't have time to get to that yet. Now I had three names: Daze, Ghost and Shawn. By the end of the day, I planned to catch up with one, if not all of them, and accelerate their journey to a shallow grave.

Chapter Nineteen

~ Sunday

Katie's mouth opened wide and she cooed, making a sound that only God's angels could mimic, before closing her eyes. I smiled as I stared at her dreamily, feeling my heart dwell with the unconditional love that I felt for my baby girl. I'd just finished nursing, bathing, dressing her and then I sang a sweet song to her to get her ready for bed. It was our nighttime ritual and worked like a charm every time.

Katie was a sweet baby. Once I got her to sleep, she wouldn't wake up until the morning. When I thought about it, it was insane to me how much I'd taken to being a mother in such a short amount of time. Even with Caesar not helping me at all with her, I was okay. I hated that he would never be the father she needed, but I knew that I had more than enough of what it took to do everything on my own. All I could do was hope that, one day, he'd come around.

Just as I was placing Katie down in her bed, there was a knock at the front door and I sighed, rolling my eyes. Just like clockwork, here was Caesar deciding to come by when all the work was done. He never came around until he knew Katie was in bed and, even then, he only came to beg me for sex or try to rub up on my ass. I was sick of it. Even though I was more than ready for some dick, I'd be damned if I got some from a nigga who hadn't done a thing for our daughter since the day that she'd breathed her first breath.

"Caesar, you need to find somewhere else to go because—"

My words caught in my throat when I snatched open the door and realized that the face that I was looking into was not Caesar's.

"King?"

I gasped and took a moment to scan the street behind him before pulling him inside by the arm. For the last few nights, a patrol car had been stationed on the corner and I was convinced it was watching to see if King would come by and visit me. I couldn't prove it, but I felt like someone had seen him when he came over to drop me and Katie off at the hospital.

"What are you *doin'* here? A cop has been here every day this week and—"

Once again, I stopped talking, but it was because of the look on King's face. He seemed stone cold in demeanor, possibly angry, at something or someone. Was it me?

"Sunday, I don't want to do this to you, but I have no other choice."

My blood went cold and I found myself taking a few steps back away from him. My breathing accelerated and I suddenly became aware of the fact that I was in a room, alone, with a man who had killed before and looked like he was ready to kill again. I was just about ready to scream when, suddenly, King lifted his hand. I closed my eyes to brace myself for what would come next.

"Are these the men who almost killed you? Do you recognize any of them?"

Confused, I pried my eyes open slowly and relaxed when I saw that he was only holding up a cell phone. Then I tensed up again when I brought into focus the images on the screen.

"My God!"

With my hands over my mouth, I felt tears streaming from my eyes. On the phone was a photo of three men who were bound, bloody and beaten to nearly a pulp. There was no telling how much torture they'd been through, but it was enough to bring them almost to death's door. Of the three men, neither of them could sit up on their own; they were being held up by anonymous hands for the photo.

"Sunday, I need you to try to remember. It's important. Are these the right men?"

I didn't want to, but I managed to force my eyes open slowly, wincing as I stared at the sight. It was hard to make out any distinguishing features on any of the faces, but there was something that drew me to one.

"I know him," I whispered and slowly lifted my hand.

I couldn't even bring myself to touch the screen, so I simply hovered over the image of the man with the green eyes.

"He's the one who shot me."

Without even bothering to look at the image, King pulled another phone from his pocket and dialed a number. While he waited for the other line to be answered, he kept his eyes on me. I folded my arms around my body, feeling like I was going to lose my mind.

"Finish it," was all he said, but it was more than enough. By the time he ended the call and placed the phone back in his pocket, I knew it was over.

"It's done."

The moment he let those two words escape from his lips, it was like I couldn't hold back my emotions any longer. All of the tears, frustration and emotions that I'd held back for so long came to the surface and I let them out.

Outside of what I felt for my daughter, I'd pushed everything else away—my anger with Caesar, the guilt that I felt when it came to King and my depression when it came to the lack of control I had over my life. I never even took the time to mourn all the things I'd lost: my life, my eye, my home, my feeling of security, even Kirk, my friend. All of those emotions began to pour out of me, and I was at a loss for how to control it. Before I knew it, I was in King's arms and he was kissing the top of my head while rubbing my back.

"This ain't the time for tears. It's all good now," he said, trying to calm me. "I took care of it. I'll always take care of you. Never forget that."

At some point between crying about what I'd lost, King flipped the script and started reminding me of all that I had to gain. Everything that could be mine if I wanted it. He went from rubbing my back to running his hands over the curve of my ass, cupping it possessively as my tears began to subside. I lifted my head to him and looked deeply into his eyes. He didn't turn away and, in that moment, we began speaking to each other though there were no words said. It was better that way; I was letting my heart do the talking. Making decisions with my mind had cost me a lot of time already. Had I followed my heart from the beginning, I wouldn't have ever left King; he would still be mine.

King lowered his head to suck gently on my bottom lip and I allowed him to, not returning the kiss until he pulled me closer into him. I sucked in a breath and he took advantage, forcing his tongue into my mouth. Tasting him brought back memories that I'd fought hard to forget after I'd caught Makita visiting him in prison. My heart was broken, and I tried to erase myself of everything King-related memory.

He dipped his hand further down, nudging the hem of my short dress aside and dipped his fingers into my pussy, working me slowly before speeding up the pace. I parted my thighs, giving him extra room to do his thing. And he did it so well...

"I need you," I heard myself say. I was so wet that as he fingered me, the sounds of the motion could be heard, arousing me even the more. Reaching down, I satisfied my curiosity as to whether he was just as horny as I was in that moment and grabbed his dick.

God...

It was long, thick and hard; just like I remembered it. My lady lips contracted, gushing even more honey from my folds.

"I want to apologize in advance," he said, suddenly, whispering against my lips, working each word in between his kisses. "I haven't felt pussy since the last time I was inside you. It's been a long time."

His confession sent tingles down my spine. I felt honey gush from between my legs.

"And you're apologizin' for that?"

"No," he said, shaking his head. "I'm apologizin' because I might be a little rough."

With fair warning given, he lifted me up and simultaneously snatched at my lace panties tearing them in two. Driving backwards, he forced my back against the wall behind us and before I had a chance to prepare myself, he gripped hard on my sides and dove straight into my middle.

"Shit, *King*!" I exclaimed, gnashing my teeth as I fought to adjust to his girth.

He was savage with it, and it didn't take long for me to understand why he'd apologized. King had always been a gentle lover, but not in this moment. The craziest part about it was that I loved every bit of it.

Stifling my scream by biting hard on his shoulder, I gripped him as he drove inside of me, building out my insides to be his custom fit.

Caesar could never compare to King. In all ways, he was much less, even when it came to his dick.

"I missed this … I promise you, I missed it."

I didn't have to let him know that I felt the same way because, truthfully, my body was saying it for me. I was so wet to the point that I was nearly leaking. My pussy was making it rain.

Out of need and his sensitivity from abstaining for so long, King came fast and so did I, but as soon as the first one was out of the way, he slowed it down. We were so caught up in the moment that we never took the time to make it to the room or the bed. Our surroundings was the least of our worries, my focus was on him and his was on me. He rocked my body, kissing me sweetly as he pulled me into ecstasy. We stayed face-to-face and when we came together for the second time, it was such an emotional moment that I almost cried.

"I want you to come with me. You and Katie," he said once it was over.

With our clothes half on and half off, we lay on the floor looking at the ceiling with the crowns of our head touching each other's. Our arms up, with our palms resting on our shoulders and our fingers were laced together.

"Come with you?" I frowned. "Where? What do you mean?"

"I'm goin' to Cuba. Tonight. The only thing keeping me here this long was finding the men who hurt you."

My expression steeled and I felt like a boulder had been forced between us.

"Cuba? Tonight? Why didn't you tell me that before now?"

"I wasn't sure that I was leavin' until now. When you told me that you recognized the men in the picture, I decided then. It's too risky for me to stay. The Feds are on the hunt for me, I can't trust anyone and—"

"I didn't tell them about you that day. I heard on the news that someone called them, but it wasn't me."

"I know," he replied without missing a beat. "I don't know who did, but I know it wasn't you."

Silenced passed between us and I forced myself to enjoy it. These were our last moments. King wanted me to go with him but we both knew there was no way. My mother was here, Katie's doctors were here, and there was no way I could take her away from her father. Even if Caesar hadn't gotten it together enough to be the father that Katie deserved, he was still present and had the opportunity to change. If I left, he'd never get that chance.

"I can't go with you," I told him, voicing the inevitable. "There is just so much here that I can't leave. My mama and…"

I didn't want to mention Caesar to King.

"I knew you would say that," he replied. "But the offer is there, and it stands. If at any point you change your mind, just know I'll always find a way to bring you to me."

The emphatic and confident way he put those words together took my breath away.

"I've got to go. My phone is probably blowing up… I've been here too long."

He pulled his hands away from mine and started to get himself together. It wasn't like him to fuck and leave, that was one thing King never did, but I didn't feel slighted at all. I knew he was leaving because he had to; the way he stared longingly at me as he fixed his clothes let me know that, if he could have it any other way, he would stay.

"Shower before you go?" I asked, biting down on my bottom lip.

He stopped just as he pulled his sweats to his waist and leveled his eyes on me.

"Of course."

With his lips pressed against mine, King carried me into the bathroom, turning on the shower without once breaking our embrace. When the temperature was just how he knew I liked it, he first peeled off my clothes, then his, and we both stepped in. We made love tenderly in the way that we used to when we knew we had all the time in the world to enjoy each other. Although we were working on borrowed time, King never made me feel like he had to rush. He was a man who had wasted so much time in prison, serving time for a crime he didn't commit, so he understood that every moment was one to be cherished.

"I love you, Sunday," he said to me as we stood at the front door.

I fought back my tears and tried to convince myself that this wasn't a 'goodbye'. If I accepted that, I would hate myself every day for not leaving with him.

"I love you too, Malik," I replied.

His eyes lit up with hope, but I couldn't say what he wanted me to. He wanted me to agree to leave, but I couldn't. Opening the door, I took a deep breath as I watched him step over the threshold for the very last time. It was dark out and the streets were, thankfully, vacant.

Leaning in one last time, he kissed my lips one more time and then wrapped his arms around my body, pulling me close.

"If you change your mind, text me and let me know. I'll come back for you. I promise."

The words were right at the tip of my tongue, but I kept my silence. My selfishness told me that I needed to leave, but it wasn't just about me. I had Katie and my mama to think of.

Standing at the door, I watched as King got into his car and prepared to leave. He kept his head down, not once looking back in my direction. When he left, I stood there and watched his car until it disappeared down the road and turned the corner. Once that happened, the tears I'd been holding in began to fall down my cheeks. With a heavy exhale, I rubbed the tears from my eyes and started to close the door but hesitated when I saw movement across the street. I gasped when I saw a shadowy figure in the distance, like someone had been watching me.

Caesar?

Squinting, I tried to focus in on whatever or whoever it was in the distance but, after a while, I realized there was no one there.

Maybe I imagined it, I thought, closing the door.

Even still, I locked it and made sure to turn on the alarm as well. I wasn't taking any chances.

Chapter Twenty

~
King

It has been a minute since I'd been able to visit my mom's house. I'd seen her a few times since I'd escaped from prison, but never at her house. Being that I was on the run, I couldn't take the risk. My mom's crib was the first place that the Feds would expect to find me at, so I avoided it altogether. Instead of visiting her there, I would pop up at random times in different locations when she least expected it. I had someone watching her residence at all times, so I knew when she was home and, when she left, I knew where she was going.

My mama lived on six acres in Roswell, Georgia. It cost a pretty penny to get that much land so close to the city, but I sprung for it without a second thought. When I had her house built, I made sure to have a secret entrance built that wasn't part of any of the floorplans available for the property. No matter where I went or how many homes I bought, the one my mama lived in would forever be home base, a refuge for me when I desperately needed it.

This night I was using that secret entrance because I had to see her. For all I knew, it could be the last time she laid eyes on me for a very long time.

There was a house about a mile away from my mama's crib, a small shack that looked like it probably belonged to a lady who lived inside with twenty cats. The entrance to the secret entrance to my mom's crib was in the closet in the master bedroom of that shack. Once inside, you entered a long underground hallway that dead-ended at a staircase that allowed entry into my mom's backyard. There was a key to her back door in the shed, but only I knew it was there.

With the key in hand, I unlocked the back door and stepped inside, right I through the kitchen.

"What in the world?"

It was my mama's voice. Standing completely still, I waited for her to come and investigate. One thing I'd taught her was to always stay strapped, so she had enough guns stashed in her house to supply a small army.

"Ma, it's me," I said, to avoid a bullet directly to the gut.

"Malik?"

"King, is that you?"

I frowned deeply. I definitely wasn't expecting the second voice.

Before I could answer, my moms came from around the corner with Makita right behind her.

What is she doin' here? I thought, looking hard at her.

"Malik! My god, boy!" she exclaimed and ran over to me. She wrapped me in her arms and held me tight like it was the first time since I'd escaped death row.

"Makita was telling me 'bout how important it was for you to leave. She said that the Feds came to her house lookin' for you. She showed up here askin' where you were, and I got so scared when she told me why. You weren't answerin' your phone… I was so scared!"

I cut my eyes at Makita, unable to shield her from the fury in my eyes. I'd always been clear about leaving my mama out of things because I didn't want her to worry. Makita telling my mom's about the

Feds at her crib was a power play; she was doing everything she could to convince me that I needed to skip town and now she had my mama on her side.

"Ma, I need to talk to you for a moment. Let's go out back."

Ignoring Makita's presence, I wrapped my arm around my mama's shoulders and ushered her out to the back deck. There was something about Makita that I just didn't trust. She'd always been loyal and, for as much as I could tell, she'd never done me wrong, but my instincts were telling me differently. A jealous woman could be the ruin of a man and Makita was exactly that. It was no secret that I was in love with Sunday and that I would always be.

When Makita first showed up at the prison to see me, I'd told her that then and she'd convinced me that it wasn't a factor to her. According to what she told me, her sole intentions were to get me out, to help me avoid a death sentence for a crime that I didn't commit. She started to smuggle drugs into the prison for me to deal on the inside so I could make money while I was locked up. She had no idea that I'd been sending every dollar back to Sunday. In fact, she had no idea that Sunday and I were still together.

Makita would come to visit me and pass the drugs over through a kiss. One of the guards was in on the scheme so he would pretend to look away so we could make the exchange. Makita would tongue-kiss me with so much passion that I knew it was more about the kiss than the drugs for her; she was enjoying herself. Then one day, Sunday suddenly stopped visiting me and I was devastated. I made the mistake of venting about my heartache to Makita and she swooped in to stake claim on me once again. I flirted with her every now and then, said things I knew she wanted to hear, but it was only because I needed her company. With Sunday gone, I didn't want to be left completely alone.

"Ma, I gotta leave. Tonight," I started once we were outside. "You already know that if you want to come with me, I can—"

"No," she said, shaking her head. "I know you have to leave, and I will miss you more than you'll ever know, but I can't." She spoke with strength in her voice, but there were tears in her eyes.

"Your sister—Nikki—she has those two babies to take care of and I'm the only one helpin' her with them since their father was killed."

Looking back at my moms, I didn't blink an eye. I knew that she, and Nikki, both suspected that me and The JDBs were behind the murder after Nikki's baby daddy snitched on me. We were, but I'd never admit it.

"You didn't offer to bring your sister along. Is something going on between you two? You know she asked Andre not to talk to the police. She hated that he did that, but she had to forgive him for the sake of the kids. He was their daddy."

I couldn't respond how I wanted, and I knew my mama would never understand how I felt. My attitude now and forever would be "Fuck Andre". May he rest in piss.

Hood rules said that you didn't snitch, period. Why should I give a damn that he was my niece and nephews father when he didn't give a damn about lying to give their uncle a death sentence? That muthafucka didn't even snitch with the truth; he made up some shit for the Feds to use against me. That was slimy, no matter how you split it.

"A nigga who knows the ones that tried to kill Sunday said that someone close to me, a chick, was fucking the nigga who set me up and ordered the hit on her and her baby daddy as some kind of revenge kill or some shit. The only person I can think of who fits that criteria is Nikki. I haven't heard from her since I been free. I know she blames me for what happened to Andre."

My mama lifted a brow. "Should she?"

I didn't answer.

LEO SULLIVAN

"Listen to me. Nikki is hurt, and she will get over that in her own time, but she doesn't blame you. If anything, she blames Andre. He brought this on himself and she knows that. It's just hard for her to see you because she feels guilty and angry at the same time. Give her some space and she will come around. But you're her blood and she loved Sunday—so do I. She would never try to kill her or her unborn child because of what happened to Andre."

It sounded good, but I would need more than a mother's words in defense of her only daughter to persuade me. My mama was loyal to her kids and I knew that better than anyone. As much shit as I'd pulled in my life and she still showed up at my appeal, hollering like I was innocent.

"I love you, ma. You know that stash I left here? It's enough money for you to live off of, so you'll be good for life. I also want to put some to the side for Sunday. She's too proud to get it right now, but she will come around when she needs it."

My mama looked at me, trying to keep her face straight but she couldn't hide her smile.

"My darling, Sunday. I would have hoped that she were the one you would have chosen to fly away with you instead of that raggedy-tail girl in my living room."

Scoffing, she rolled her eyes. She could play nice, but the truth was that she'd never liked Makita, not even a little bit. Sunday had always been her favorite and they formed a bond the second they met for the first time. Honestly, they had a lot in common. Maybe the old adage about a man choosing a woman like his mother was true.

"I wanted to," I admitted, feeling a throbbing sensation erupt in the center of my chest. "I just left her; I asked her to come with me, but she couldn't."

Somehow, saying she *couldn't* felt better than admitting that she *wouldn't.*

My mama stared back at me with compassionate eyes. Although I was hiding my hurt, she could read me like a book. I wasn't the typical thug who was void of emotion and ran the streets with cold, calculated ways birthed out of his inability to love. I'd always known how to love because since the moment I'd met her, I'd loved Sunday.

"You know Sunday is a lot like me, maybe that's partly why you picked her." She laughed a little with her joke. "But what I mean is, she's used to sacrificing her needs for the needs of others. It's going to be hard to convince her to leave her mother here and even harder to convince her to tear that baby away from her father."

Against my will, I felt my facial expression harden.

"And yes, I know he ain't shit as a father, but Sunday is going to keep hope alive that he will come around because she thinks it's best for her daughter at the moment. Once she realizes the mistake she's making, I hope it won't be too late."

I shook my head. "It won't ever be too late. Not for her."

Sadness rimmed my mama's eyes, but she managed to smile through it.

"At some point, you will have to move on. We both have to. As much as you love her, she's doing what is best for her and you have to do what is best for you."

With a clenched jaw, I respectfully listened but I wasn't accepting it. Sunday and I had a connection that transcended the normal things that kept people together. True, she was a woman and she liked to be loved and paid attention to, which opened the door for Caesar's bum ass to creep in when I let her down, but the connection was still there.

"When everything dies down, I'll send a way for you to come visit me. Nikki, too," I added just for her benefit.

"You know I'll come. I'll be happy to see you."

***

"You're leaving her... Are you leaving me too?"

With Makita behind me, I stopped in my tracks and glanced up at the starry night sky. This was the conversation that I'd been trying to avoid, which is why I'd opted to slip out before Makita was able to discover that I was gone. Unfortunately, her awareness of everything around her was a fine-tuned trait. It was one yet another thing that she'd learned from me.

"I'm leavin' everyone," I replied with a sigh before turning around. "I only came to say bye."

"Not to *her*. You didn't say goodbye to *her*, did you? You wanted her to come along. To join you."

There was no doubt in my mind that the *her* she was talking about wasn't my mama.

She took a few paces forward, looking like the average man's version of heaven on Earth. Makita was drop dead gorgeous and I should feel honored that a woman of her caliber would be so intent on being with me, but I couldn't force feelings that I didn't have. I valued her, I was loyal to her, but I didn't love her. Not how she wanted me to, and I never would.

"Why can't you be honest with me, King? You still love Sunday and you always will. There is no room in your heart for me."

She blew out a breath and I watched as she tried to compose herself. This revelation was hurting her, but I wouldn't lie in order to put her at ease. In a few hours, I would be gone so it was best for her to know the truth.

"We may not ever have what you have with her, but at least you know that with you is where I want to be... Where I will choose to be. Don't leave without taking me with you, King. You're leaving, but you don't have to be alone. I can help you build what we have over here in any location. I'm hood bred, like Jay Z. Put me anywhere on God's green Earth and I'll triple my worth."

She giggled and then wiped a tear from her right cheek. For a moment as I looked at her, I considered what she was saying and I was about to agree to it, but then stopped to reconsider.

"Makita, I can't do that. To take you with me would be the selfish thing to do. You've already waited on me for so long, put your life on hold without knowing what my fate would be... I can't ask you to do that again. I wouldn't take you with me just so you can wait around for me to give you what you want from me. Whenever Sunday becomes an option, everything else for me stops. We could be together for ten years and the moment Sunday resurfaces, if she says that she wants me, I'll drop everything and anyone to pursue that. You deserve a man who will do that for you."

Her expression crumbled; she was overcome with so much emotion that she couldn't speak, but I considered it a blessing. Turning away, I continued on the trail to the secret passageway in the shed.

"King, wait."

Running my hand over the top of my head, I turned around.

"Yeah?"

"Can you do one thing?" she began to ask. "Can you tell me where you hid your part of the shipment from the Colombians? Since you're leaving, I can flip it for you. I'll send you your normal percentage, of course. Just tell me where to—"

I shook my head. "No."

That wasn't at all what she'd been expecting. She jerked her neck back and frowned.

"Why? Are you taking it with you?"

"No, I'm selling it back to the Colombians for whatever they decide to give me, just so I can get it off my hands. Then I'm donating the money to research on autism and prelingual deafness."

The fire in Makita's eyes showed that she was fully aware as to why I was donating the money to those subjects specifically. I didn't know how, but she was aware of the issues surrounding Sunday's child.

"It's always about her, huh?"

I didn't reply; no need to pour salt on an open wound. In the end, I was sure she knew the answer: Of course.

In my mind, Sunday was, will be and just *is*. Everything was always about her.

Chapter Twenty-One

Sunday

I was uptight. My nerves were getting the best of me. Behind me, my mama was making something that smelled like eggs. The sound of whatever utensil she was using, scraping against the frying pan, made me want to scream. I had so many thought swirling around my head that I was having the hardest time trying to make sense of even one.

"Is there something wrong?"

My mama walked in to where I was sitting at the dining room table and placed a paper plate in front of me. Holding one of her own, she slid into a chair next to me and bore her eyes into mine.

"Actually, I should say, I *know* that something is wrong, so why don't you go ahead and tell me what it is."

She lifted her pressed egg and cheese sandwich from her plate and sunk her teeth in. With her mouth full, she chewed while patiently watching me. I dropped my head down and stared at the sandwich on my plate. There was no way I could eat.

"King came by. He... He found the guys who tried to kill me and..." I swallowed and looked away, unable to figure out how to finish that sentence.

"Basically, they aren't a problem anymore," my mama finished for me.

"Right." I nodded. "But he also told me that he had to leave. He asked if I wanted to bring Katie and leave with him."

My mama stopped chewing suddenly to frown.

"Well, why are you here lookin' like somebody died? Why aren't you packin' your things?"

"Mama! You know I can't leave. I have to stay here for you and I can't take Katie away from her daddy."

"Girl, please." She rolled her eyes. "Katie's *daddy*, as you call him, has already left her, if you ask me. He don't see that child as it is. And, as for me, I'm good. I got my own life, so you need to get yours. I know you think that every night I come home late is because I'm working but that's not the case. I got me a man and we might be gettin' married if everything keeps going well."

I choked on my own saliva and began to sputter out cough.

"A man?"

"Yes, and he's a doctor. I met him at the hospital durin' all that time that I was there worried 'bout you. He helped me to relax and take my mind off things. But that's all I'll tell you because I don't wanna jinx it." She crosses her fingers for added effect. "Do you, live your life. Don't worry 'bout me."

She continued smacking on her sandwich and I allowed my mind to marinate on what she said.

Maybe she was right. Who else did I have to think about other than myself, her and Katie? Kelly and I weren't even close anymore; I guess the moment I was no longer interested in turning up or smoking weed, she no longer had time for me. When the press was around after

I was released from the hospital, she was the first one giving interviews all in the news. As soon as they left, she was gone, too.

Just as my mama stood up to clean up her plate, there was a knock at the front door.

"Let me guess," she began with a sarcastic tone. "That's your baby daddy coming to spend time with his baby now that the baby is asleep."

I didn't even have the energy to reply and wouldn't even if I did. She was right. Caesar was a waste of time and if it wasn't for Katie, I wouldn't even let him come around.

"Who in there? I heard another voice while I was waitin.'"

Staring at me from under hooded, suspicious eyes, he flexed his jaw as he waited for me to respond. I was so sick of this jealous streak he had developed. He didn't own me.

"What do you mean? That's my mama! She lives here, remember?"

Caesar pushed by me forcefully, letting himself into the house as if he belonged there. I closed the door and locked it, already agitated by his mere presence. Dragging my feet up under me, I followed in the direction that he'd gone and was further annoyed when I saw him sitting at the table, chewing on the sandwich my mama had made for me.

"Sunday, I'm goin' to bed. I'll get up to get my grand baby when she wakes up in the morning."

My mama put extra emphasis on a few of her words and cut her eyes hard at Caesar as she spoke.

"You don't see me sittin' here?" he shouted so loud that I flinched.

"Caesar!"

"My eyes don't see nobody that my grand baby don't see," my mama replied, matching his aggression with a dose of petty. She put an extra swish in her hips and sashayed to her room.

"That bitch gettin' besides herself," Caesar grumbled.

I blinked hard, knowing for sure that I had not heard what I thought I had.

"Excuse me? I know you didn't just—"

Before I could finish the sentence, something began to ring. It was a phone, but I was confused. It wasn't mine.

"That yours?" Caesar asked, noting the confusion on my face.

"No, it must be mama's."

That theory failed in the next moment when she opened her door and yelled, "Sunday, get that phone before you wake up that baby!"

"Either you lyin' or somebody left they phone over here. Which is it?"

My throat felt like it was closing. If a phone had been left, it could only be King's. But he hadn't gone anywhere outside of the living room and the ringing was coming from my bedroom. I didn't understand.

With Caesar hot on my heels, I took off down the hall and turned the room light on dim to find the source of the ringing. It didn't take long for me realize that it was coming from the small box with the bow on top, the gift box that King had brought over for me. Though I'd opened the box he brought over for Katie, an electric rocker, I wasn't able to open the one for me and I placed it on the top shelf of my closet instead.

I could feel Caesar's heated stare on my back as I stood up on my toes and reached for it. Once I'd ripped the wrapping paper off, I pulled the top off of the box and noticed a small ring-sized box inside as well as the source of the ringing: a cell phone.

"Who bought this shit?" Caesar asked and snatched the phone from my hands.

I tried to hide my panic as I watched him go through it. There was no telling what he would see.

"Sunday, I asked you to leave with me and I understand your reasons for wanting to stay. I just want to let you know that offer will always remain. I know that right now you probably won't accept any money from me, but I set some aside for you. I want to make sure that, regardless to what happens, you and Katie are set for life. With love always, King."

Once Caesar was done reading the text message, he lifted his head and glared at me with so much hatred, the intensity and heat radiating from his eyes could probably melt metal and bones.

"So, basically, this nigga got me out in the streets, searchin' for info and shit, workin' for him when all the while, he's in the background tryin' to scoop my girl?"

Caesar reared his hand back as if he was going to smash the phone into pieces and then thought against it and slammed it hard against my forehead instead.

"You grimy bitch!"

The force of the phone against my forehead sent radiating pain shooting through my skull. I screamed and reached out for something—anything—to break my fall. My hand knocked against the door handle and I gripped it to stop from reeling backwards.

"I should kill you. You know that?"

Before I knew what was happening, Caesar had pulled a gun from his waist and had it aimed at my skull. He was standing so close to me that our noses nearly touched. My nose hairs singed at the smell of liquor on his breath. Not only was he drunk but he was high on something, I could see it in his eyes.

Percocets, I thought.

We had both been prescribed pain killers at the hospital, but I never used mine because I wasn't positive that it didn't affect my breast milk. Caesar, on the other hand, took his and mine. Now that he was in the streets again, percs and oxys were easy to get.

"Caesar, stop. I didn't do anything," I pleaded, looking from him to our daughter who was sleeping right behind him. "Our child is in here. Just chill, you're not thinkin' correctly."

"Fuck all that! I'm sick of this shit, I'm sick of playin' these games and I'm sick that muthafucka you been throwin' in my fuckin' face all these years!" He was yelling and spewing saliva into my face.

I was frozen in place by fear and scared to move a muscle. There was no doubt in my mind that Caesar wouldn't kill me. He wasn't the man I remembered him to be. Circumstances had changed the both of us, but he'd allowed them to get the best of him. I hadn't spent much time around him, so I never picked up on all of the changes in him. Either that, or I simply didn't care enough to pay attention.

"Now what you gon' do right now is hit this nigga up and tell him that you want to see him when he leaves. Then you gon' get him to tell you where he left the money he stashed for you. But before all that pop off, me and you gon' have a lil' chit-chat with the police to let them know that we found someone of interest to them."

The fetid smell of his alcohol-scented breath stung my nose hairs yet again and I winced at the sordid scent. In this moment, I was terrified about what he would do next. One thing was for sure—he was definitely out of his mind; I was sure of that. There was no way I would call the Feds on King; I couldn't be the reason for him to be locked up again.

"I'm not doing that. Caesar, you need to stop this crazy shit. I'm not callin' the cops on King and you already know that."

LEO SULLIVAN

What I had yet to realize was that Caesar had the gun, so he was holding all the cards. There was a lot that could be said about a desperate person who had been pushed into a corner, but even more could be said about one who also had a gun.

"I already know that, huh?"

His tone was sinister as he pulled away, delivering what sounded like a dry cackle. The limp in his gait was even more pronounced than it had ever been before and I wondered if his physical condition was worsening.

When he stopped next to Katie's bassinet and peered down at her with his lips twisted into an evil sneer, my breath caught in my lungs.

"Caesar, no!" I screamed and flung myself forward just as he reached over and forcefully snatched her tiny body into his rough hands.

"You think I'm kidding, don't you? You think just because you got that nigga who acts like he runs everybody checkin' for you again that I don't deserve no respect?"

With my hands over my ears, I howled to the heavens when he nudged the barrel of his gun dangerously close to Katie's head. She jumped awake and began to cry out. The sound of her painful wails only made me sob even harder.

"Caesar, please, put her down! Give her to me, please!"

"Shut the fuck up, bitch!" he raged with crazed, maniacal eyes. "I don't wanna hear shit outside of you tellin' me what da fuck I want to hear!"

"What's goin' on in here!" I heard my mama's voice behind the closed door and seconds later, she was knocking hard on it with force, as if she were trying to push it down.

"Pick up that fuckin' phone right now and hit that nigga back before he leaves and tell him what da fuck I said. Tell him you comin' up there to find out 'bout that money or I'ma bust a cap in a bitch ass!"

The air in the room was stifling but somehow, I was able to move. I wasn't sure which 'bitch' Caesar was referring to, but I was ready to risk my life for either of my two loved ones in the house, so it didn't really matter.

Just as I bent down to pick up the phone on the floor, the door to my room burst open. I glanced up and all sounds around me zeroed out into white noise when I saw the gun in her hands. She had it out, pointed right at Caesar with her finger on the trigger, ready to protect her child. Meanwhile, the only thought in my head was how in the world was I going to get over to Caesar in time to protect mine.

Boom! Boom!

Shots were fired, completely muting out the sound of me screeching to the top of my lungs. When the chaos subsided and my eyes fell into focus on Katie who was still crying her heart out in Caesar's arms, I expelled all of the air from my lungs, somewhat able to relax now that I knew my child was alive. But when I heard labored breathing at my side, my heart dropped to my feet. Slowly, I turned my head, fresh tears already falling from my eyes.

"Mommy, nooooo!" I cried out as I looked down at her.

My mama was sprawled out on the floor with two holes spilling blood from her chest. Her eyes were wide and fixated on some object above her that no eyes but her could see. It was like she didn't even know that I was there. Her eyes closed as her breaths became more jagged. I lowered my head and pressed my forehead against hers, not wanting to accept what I already knew was coming next.

"Mommy, please, don't leave me..."

Even as I said it, I knew she was gone. I'd felt the exact moment when her spirit had left. It was over. With my eyes squeezed shut, I pressed my forehead against hers, feeling her warm skin close to mine for what I knew would be the last time.

"Get da fuck up. I didn't even wanna kill that bitch, but she had it coming. You got a job to do or else I might make another mistake again."

Chapter Twenty-Two

~ King

Sunday: I want to see you before you leave. Tell me where we can meet. I just want to say bye.

The text came through as soon as my driver was pulling up to the private plane that I'd chartered to take me to Cuba. Thanks to Bulletproof and Dolo making major moves in music with The JDB crew, it had been easy to get. There were always artists and celebrities flying out of the ATL in private jets to perform internationally. No one raised an eyebrow when they set up the request.

I didn't hesitate to return Sunday's text with the address to where I was along with instructions on how to make it to where I was. My next message was to my ally who worked in airport security who would be sure that she made it back without issue. He hit me back to say that I needed to leave as soon as possible and shouldn't delay any longer, but I ignored the text.

"Something happen?"

"Nah, nothing."

Running my hand over my face, I turned to Makita and regretted that she was there. My stance on everything was still the same; I could never be the man she wanted me to be and I wouldn't pretend. Even knowing that, she was determined to be with me, and I couldn't completely understand why.

Beautiful women like Makita felt like they could change a man over time. They felt like they could mold a man into who they wanted him to be. That shit wouldn't work over here. I had my own mind and I made my own moves. At the same time, nobody wanted to be alone and I wasn't an exception to that. Sexually, Makita wasn't all that bad from what I could remember. My thought had been that it wouldn't hurt to have her around. But all that had come into play before Sunday's text.

"Somethin' has happened. I can see it all over your face," Makita shot back, pointing at me with a single lifted finger, leveled at my chest.

"Ain't shit, I just gotta handle somethin'. I'll help get your bags out and you go ahead and wait for me on the plane. Once I finish with what I gotta do, I'll be on."

She cocked her head to the side and looked at me sideways like she didn't quite believe that I'd meet her onboard. It was like she was contemplating if I would run once she got on the plane.

"You promise?"

I nodded my head. "I'll be on," I repeated.

Not too much longer after getting Makita adjusted and making sure all of our luggage had made it on, I got a text from my partner saying that a vehicle was heading to the back for me. My pulse quickened with anticipation. If I could have it my way, this wouldn't be the last time I would see Sunday. I didn't care if Makita was on the plane waiting for me. The same doors that she used to walk into the plane would be the exact same ones that she would use to make it off. I'd warned her that if Sunday gave me another chance, it was curtains on whatever she was trying to make work and I meant that.

The first thing I noticed when Sunday stepped out of the driver's seat of the car was her tear-streaked face and puffy eyes. It looked like she had been crying for hours and my senses immediately went on high alert. There was no way that her appearance right now had anything to do with me. There was no reason to feed myself the bullshit.

"What happened?" was the first thing I said when she was standing in front of me.

With her head bowed, she avoiding looking directly at me and shook her head.

"Where is Katie? She in the car or with ma?" I asked, as usual, referring to her mother in the same way I referred to mine.

I wasn't expecting it, but Sunday opened her mouth and released a sob so tormenting in nature that my chest began to throb with a devastating ache, and I didn't even know why.

She covered her mouth to silence her cries and her body suddenly went rigid. For some reason, I glanced behind her towards the car. Something about the way she was standing, positioned at a weird angle towards me, but just right to shield her face from the passenger side of the whip, alarmed me.

"Who is in the car?"

The moment the question was out, the way her body jumped to attention like she was afraid told me that I was on the right track.

"How many?" I asked, barely moving my lips.

She swallowed and answered, her voice only a notch above a whisper.

"One. And Katie," she added. "He said he would kill her. He put a gun to her head."

Fuck.

Heat built up at the base of my neck and I kept my eyes low to avoid looking back towards the car again. Katie being in the car made things complex. Had she not been in there, I would have shot up the car and made it a custom casket for Caesar's stupid ass. I knew it couldn't be nobody but a coward like him hiding in a car using his own baby as a hostage.

Suddenly, the back door of the car opened, and the air was filled with the traumatic sound of Katie's cries.

"Da fuck takin' yo' stupid ass so gotdamn long? You know we ain't got all fuckin' day." Caesar climbed out of the car with Katie wailing away in one arm and a gun in his other hand. His finger was positioned precariously close to the trigger as he spoke with a threatening tenor in his voice.

"We tried it the nice way, but I ain't got time for all that." He nudged the gun at Katie, as if pointing. "And this cryin' ass baby definitely don't got time because I'm gettin' tired of listenin' to all this whinin' and shit."

Dropping to her knees, Sunday was overcome with sobs as she collapsed helplessly to the ground. Out of instinct, my fingers flexed. My pistol was at my side, but I couldn't risk a shot while Caesar was holding Katie.

"Fuck this shit," Caesar said and then pointed his gun at Sunday.

Somehow, he was able to balance Katie in his arms just long enough to get the car door open again and toss her inside. He closed the door to mute out her cries and then began to walk closer, his gun still firmly aimed at the back of Sunday's head.

"Tell me where the money is that you said you got stashed for her. That's all I want and then I'll go. If you don't speak, I'll kill her and then hold you here at gun point while I call the Feds. Choice is yours."

"What the hell—Caesar?"

It was Makita and, even though I'd asked her to stay on the plane, she didn't listen, and I was grateful for it. The second that Caesar took his eyes off of me, I moved fast and retrieved my gun, grasping it firmly in my hands and aimed directly at him. If he didn't still have his finger on the trigger of the gun that was pointed at Sunday, he would've been taking a first-class trip straight to the grave.

"Da *fuck* you doin' with this nigga, Makita? What, he sweet-talk you a lil' bit and you fell right back into second place again, huh? You tryin' to skip out on me with a nigga who don't even want yo' dumb ass because he got his head too far up this bitch ass!"

Caesar shoved his gun even deeper into Sunday's skin. She yelped out in pain and my trigger finger applied a little more pressure.

"Caesar, shut up!" Makita yelled.

Her voice was strained, like she was trying to hold back her panic. I kept my eyes on Caesar, noting that he was becoming even more agitated, but his anger wasn't directed at me or Sunday any longer.

"You double-crossin' ass bitch! What happened to the plan you kept remindin' me to follow? I was supposed to get the girl and the money, and you were supposed to get the man. Now yo' scheming ass look like you only lookin' out for yourself. Just like last time! Did you tell King 'bout how you tried to set up Sunday?"

Everything went silent around me. Sunday lifted her head and I lowered my weapon.

"Da fuck you talkin' 'bout, man?"

Turning to Makita for answers, I waited for her to say something against the accusations we'd all heard.

"He's lying!"

"Lyin'?" Caesar repeated the word like it was disgusting to him. "Bitch, I ain't gotta lie 'bout shit."

From that point, he turned to me.

"King, I don't even like you like that but I'ma tell you what's up. Kita was fuckin' with Daze before you got locked up. You might know him as the one who raped Sunday, but y'all's history goes back further than that. That triple homicide you was locked up for? Daze did that shit, and Kita put him up to it."

A sour taste formed in the back of my throat. This shit couldn't possibly be true. Makita had spent all the time since I'd been locked up trying her hardest to get me off. Why would she have put me there just to spend so much time to let me go free?

Listening intently, I kept my eyes on Caesar as he continued.

"The plan was for him to kill them and then she would go back and rob the spot since she knew that was where you had your cash stashed. But then Sunday showed up and she changed the plan. She was the one who called the cops to get her locked up. Kita never suspected that you would take the charge instead."

I could vividly remember Makita telling me about how insane she thought it was for me to take the charge for Sunday.

"*No one ever does that,*" she had told me. "*The dope man's wife is supposed to know that's part of the risk of being in that position. If anyone goes down for shit, it has to be her and not you. You're the big fish; you'd get real time and she would only get a slap on the wrist. Why would you take these charges for her, King? You shouldn't have done this.*"

"You never questioned her loyalty? Why she held you down the whole time?" Caesar chuckled menacingly. "The bitch felt guilty. That was the only reason. She's responsible for setting a lot of innocent muthafuckas up. You... Gunner... Well, I gave up his name to fuck with Kita, but she knew he was innocent and let you kill him anyway. Her and Daze was staging robberies of your trap houses and blamed the shit on him so they could pocket the extra cash. Shotti knew, but he too scary to say shit which is the only reason he's still alive."

Devastated, I hung my head. Gunner was innocent; It didn't even really come as a shock because I *felt* that something was off about the whole thing. He told me not to trust Makita, and when I looked back at everything, she was the common denominator when it came to everything. The tips to the police of my location only happened when I had visited Sunday; I would bet that she was behind them, too. According to her, the Feds has burst into her home looking for me, but no one but her has seen them. In fact, that was when she really started putting pressure on me to leave and take her with me. She was behind it all.

The sound of sirens could be heard in the distance. I looked up and saw a caravan of cars with blue and red flashing lights. The police had been alerted and they were heading this way.

"Fuck! I knew I was running out of time. Enough of this shit." Caesar renewed his attention on me and pointed his gun back at Sunday. "You need to talk fast and tell me where you got that money stashed—"

Kaboom!

Caesar's head jerked back, his eyes spread wide with shock. Looking down, he blinked in disbelief when he saw the bloody hole in the center of his chest. Sunday clung to my legs for dear life, trembling ferociously. Her head was pointed away from him and I was gracious for that. The tortured stare in his eyes when he realized that he wouldn't make it out of this moment with his life, was haunting.

Pivoting fast, I lifted my gun, aimed it, and closed my eyes before pulling the trigger twice.

Boom! Boom!

"Uh!" Makita groaned loudly before doubling over and falling from the stairs to the ground below. I had no doubt that she was still alive, but I couldn't waste any time.

"Sunday, come with me. Go get Katie and let's go. You don't have a lot of time to decide."

Her eyes were fearful, but the decision was made, I could see that. After only a few seconds she nodded her head and the weight lightened in my chest. Turning quickly, she ran to retrieve her daughter and I waited for her to return so that I could help her into the plane.

"We got you ready to take off," a man I didn't recognize said as he walked up to me with another behind him. They were definitely JDB being that they didn't flinch at the sight of Caesar's body lying on the ground or Makita who was painfully panting on the other side.

"We will take care of the bodies. Steve is holding the police off for as long as he can, but you gotta go now!"

This time, I didn't have to be told twice.

With Sunday and Katie safely on the plane, all that was left now was for me to join them. The life I'd wanted to live for so long was finally within my grasp.

"Caesar, please."

Makita's pain-filled voice stopped me in my tracks. For a moment, I considered letting her live, but the reality was that I couldn't do that. She was too smart and too ruthless. Her hatred for Sunday was too strong. As long as she was alive, I couldn't be certain that she wouldn't set her mind in finishing the destruction that she'd started.

Aiming my gun, I pulled the trigger and let off a shot right in the center of her forehead. A privately hired stewardess closed the door behind me just as I boarded the plane and the pilot announced that he was preparing for take-off. As we tore down the runway, I took a second to look outside the window at the scene outside. The police cars had finally made it through to the back and were speeding down the long road that led to where we'd been only a few minutes before.

Once the plane lifted into the sky, I slid the shade down and closed my eyes, forcing myself to relax.

"It's over now," Sunday whispered, grabbing my hand into hers.

When I lifted my head, I was greeted by her sad eyes. There was a smile on her face, but it wasn't genuine. It couldn't be after all that she'd lost, and it would be a while before she would find complete happiness again. Providing that would be my new goal in life.

"It is," I replied and squeezed her hand.

It was a lie. I still had some unfinished business to tend to but, in this moment, I was going to push all of that aside and simply enjoy the ride.

Epilogue

~

One Year Later

A gentle breeze flowed through the trees and tickled the tips of Katie's nose, making her giggle as she lay on her back, observing her own chubby feet. With a smile on her lips, Sunday watched her daughter's amazement at her body, loving her innate awareness of any, every and all things around her. Katie was such a blessing in all ways. She brought joy to every room that she was in and a smile to the face of every person blessed enough to be in her presence.

Lifting her fat hands in the air, Katie started to clap them together and squealed in glee at the eruption of her sound that she'd learned to make. After being able to hear for the first time, she became preoccupied with sound and loved to experiment with all the different noises she could make. As soon as they were settled into Cuba, King made Katie one of his first priorities. There were few limits to what money could buy and, somehow, King still had an awful lot of it.

The best pediatric specialists in the world were flown in to treat Katie's ears and they made several judgments on what could be done to repair her hearing. For weeks, King and Sunday listened to presentation after presentation of doctors sharing their findings while making suggestions as to what could work to remedy the issue. In the end, the selected the surgeon who was not only one of the most qualified for the job, but who had also taken a deep and personal love for Katie during the time she'd examined her. Although she wasn't the doctor with the most accolades, it was apparent that she loved the little girl and as Sunday told King, not many things could rival love.

"Sunday, I don't know what you feedin' this little boy, but he is heavy as hell! Big babies must run in your side of the family because King and Nikki were never this big."

King's mother, who had told everyone to refer to her as Glam-Ma Joe, smacked her lips as she walked onto the back deck holding her newest grandbaby in her arms. Malik, Jr., affectionately known to his family as M.J., was only three months old and looked like an exact replica of his father.

"I'm still breastfeeding. He's not eating real food yet," Sunday spoke up, finally tearing her eyes away from her daughter to look up at her son. He was in full recline in his grandmother's arms with one fat leg hanging off to the side.

"His ass must be greedy, like his daddy. It don't make no sense for a baby this young to be this damn big at only three months. His heavy ass need to learn how to walk soon."

Giggling, Sunday rolled her eyes and watched as her mother-in-law took a seat next to her. The funny thing about it was that they had more than enough rockers, mats and blankets for M.J. to be placed in, but his grandma refused to put him down. She could complain all she wanted about how big a baby he was and how hard it was to hold him; the facts were that she wouldn't have it any other way.

Lifting her head, Sunday took a moment to stare at the setting sun and then half-turned to look behind her. Her right hand was perched on top of her stomach, rubbing her growing belly. She was pregnant, yet again, but she loved it. As her mother-in-law stated, she was a baby making machine and motherhood agreed with her. Her greatest joys in life were the moments when she was preparing to bring an unborn child into the world, and she loved every single second that followed. As soon as her six weeks were up after M.J's birth, King ended up getting her pregnant again. After spending so much time wanting it to happen and being devastated each time that life was lost, it seemed selfish to limit her body by using birth control. At some point, she would, but that was not a necessity now.

"Where is that son of yours anyways? He's about to miss our favorite part of the day," she said, still searching for King.

"Inside. He was on a call, speakin' to Bullethead or whatever his name is."

Sunday choked on her giggles. "You mean, Bulletproof?"

Glam-Ma Joe rolled her eyes. "Girl, I don't know. Yeah, him or whatever his name is."

***

With his eyes on everyone in the world who mattered most to him, King stood inside the large estate that he'd purchased for his growing family with his phone in hand. Bulletproof and Dolo were taking turns, talking a mile a minute, as they filled him in on everything that was going on back stateside with The JDB. He was happy for them, but he was only half-listening. As he looked at his family, the only thing he could think about was how grateful he was to be granted this part of his life.

"We *all* legit now, nigga!" Dolo was saying as Bulletproof laughed in the background. "This music shit is makin' more money than that street shit ever did. We doin' shows damn near every night, muthafuckas flyin' us from city-to-city, everybody want a piece of JDB."

"Yeah, shit been crazy, dog!" Bulletproof cut in. "I ain't slept in like four days. I'm hype as fuck on this lean. Shit… I wasn't supposed to tell you that but anyways—I'm just tryin' to say I stay lit!"

Laughing to himself, King shook his head. Later on, he would warn them to calm it down so they didn't get lost out there while they were living like rock stars, but that would be a lesson for another day. They were young, rich and felt invincible. What they were doing now was a natural phase of life. For the moment, he was just happy that they were no longer in the streets.

"Yo, King, we got a gift for you, man. From the intel I just got, it should arrive in five, four, three, two…"

Ding, dong!

"One! There it go," both men said in unison.

"The fuck y'all niggas been up to? This better not be no shifty lookin' nigga at my door," King joked as he walked out to the front.

"*Hell nah*, you know we don't play like that. It's JDB all day, baby. We wouldn't send nobody out there who ain't on the team."

"Fa sho," Dolo said, joining in.

King took a moment to check out the peephole and saw a black man standing outside, dressed in a suit and holding a large box in his hands. He wasn't someone he'd ever seen before but, on Bulletproof and Dolo's word, he opened the door.

"Mr. Shields, this is a delivery from The JDB," the man said as soon as he saw King's face. "Before showing you the contents inside, I want to first let you know that I have the utmost respect for you and I have pledged my life to you, my blood and my team. JDB forever."

With a nod and a straight face, King acknowledged his words and then stepped back for the box to be opened. The man grabbed at the top, pulled it back and King took in a sharp breath once he saw what was inside.

There were two heads: Daze and Shotti's.

The night that he'd shown Sunday the faces on his phone, he had been prepared to also let her know that he hadn't been able to find

Daze as of yet but seeing her break down made him change her mind. Though he knew that he would make sure no harm came to her and vowed to get up with Daze as soon as he got comfortable enough to show his face again, he couldn't leave and allow her to live every day until then in fear.

After they left for Cuba, King then discovered that Shotti had knowledge of not only the robberies but everything that Makita was doing, even though he had no parts in it. Regardless of him being involved or not, knowing about it made him just as guilty.

"Thank you," King said to the man and nodded again before closing the door.

"Merry Christmas, man!" Bulletproof's cheerful voice erupted from the phone speaker.

"Nigga, it's July," Dolo replied.

"So what? Nigga, you a hater! Since we ain't get him nothing last year, this can be for last Christmas and this one coming."

"Y'all niggas wild," King said, chuckling to himself.

Ending the call with a quick goodbye, he slid the phone into his pocket and began to make his way out to the back to join his family. Since moving to Cuba, there hadn't been a single sunset that he and Sunday hadn't enjoyed together. He wouldn't break tradition.

"I love you, King," she said, leaning into him as he took his place at her side.

With his eyes on the sky, he dipped his nose down into the crown of her head and sucked in a deep breath, filling his lungs with her scent.

"And I love you, Mrs. Sunday Shields. Always have and I always will."

Note from the Author

First, I would like to thank God Almighty for blessing me with the ability to write and helping me on my literary journey. To my wife, Porscha Sterling, my sons, Alphonzo and King-King, I love you all more than life.

To my fans, I love you all! I try to respond to every last one of the comments, messages and emails that I receive. It doesn't take much to make a brotha or sista smile and show them they are appreciated.

To the authors signed to LSP, thank you all for being some of the hardest working in the game. Your motivation, determination and drive fuels me.

Please leave me a review and let me know what you thought about this book. I love to read your thoughts. Make sure to check out the LiT Reading App and my website, www.leolsullivan.com to stay up-to-date on everything that is going on with me and my work.

Until we meet again, God bless.

Leo Sullivan

Connect with U(s)

Visit us online at
KensingtonBooks.com
to read more from your favorite authors, see books
by series, view reading group guides, and more.

for sneak peeks, chances to win books and prize packs,
and to share your thoughts with other readers.

facebook.com/kensingtonpublishing
twitter.com/kensingtonbooks

Tell us what you think!
To share your thoughts, submit a review,
or sign up for our eNewsletters, please visit:
KensingtonBooks.com/TellUs.